CAPTAIN SCARLET

AND THE

MYSTERONS

CAPTAIN SCARLET

AND THE

MYSTERONS

CHRIS DRAKE AND
GRAEME BASSETT

With a foreword by Gerry Anderson

ITC
Entertainment Group

BOXTREE

First published in Great Britain in 1993 by
Boxtree Limited

© 1993 ITC Entertainment Group Ltd
Licensed by Copyright Promotions Ltd

The right of Chris Drake and Graeme Bassett to be identified as Authors of this Work
has been asserted by them in accordance with the
Copyright, Designs and Patents Act 1988.

10 8 6 4 2   3 5 7 9

Designed by Millions Design
Typeset by SX Typesetting Ltd, Rayleigh, Essex.
Printed and bound in Scotland by Cambus Litho Limited

Boxtree Limited
Broadwall House
21 Broadwall
London SE1 9PL

A CIP catalogue entry for this book
is available from the British Library.

ISBN 1 85283 403 X

CONTENTS

Acknowledgements

Thanks to: Alan Howard and Pete Walker for lending us valuable reference material; Graham Bleathman for his extensive help with research; Katie Runciman and Lynn Simpson for checking the manuscript; Gerry and Mary Anderson, Christine Glanville, Bob Bell, Alan Pattillo, Alan Perry, Francis Matthews, Elizabeth Morgan, Gary Files, Ed Bishop, Alan Fennell, Angus Allen, Milton Finesilver, David Nightingale, Ken Cameron, Ken Scrivener, Douglas Hurring, Anvil Films Ltd, Dr George Sik of Saville & Holdsworth Ltd, Douglas Luke, Andrew Pixley, Sam Mitchell, Andy Allard, Roy A. Wright and Mitch Ross (who really is indestructible!) for advice and encouragement; Stephen Brown and Chris Bentley of FAB magazine for unearthing the 'pilot' script; Ian Boyce of Fanderson; Frank Ratcliffe and Jon Keeble at ITC Entertainment; Anthony McKay, Mike Richardson and Annette Buckley of *Time Screen* magazine; Alan Gregory of the British Film Institute; Phil Willis for advice on merchandise; Joe Dunn for lending us his models; Krystyna Zukowska for believing we could write it, and Mr P Bassett, Mr W Reid and Mr & Mrs I K Drake for all their help, tolerance and support.

Finally, thanks to P A Davy for photographing the merchandise and Lynn West for the photograph of Gerry Anderson.

Foreword by
Gerry Anderson

The significance of *Captain Scarlet* for me was that it was a major turning point in the development of Supermarionation. It was the first series in this genre where the puppets were correctly scaled with human proportions.

The result was very realistic looking puppets – so realistic that one expected them to behave like real people, and of course for many children they did. For the puppeteers, however, it meant every move had to be perfectly executed and the art department had to make the miniature sets with even greater detail than in previous shows.

The audience was split. There were those who preferred the Thunderbird puppets because they felt they were caricatures, and that's what they wanted – escapism from the real world. Then there were those who were Scarlet fans because they preferred the new realism.

At the time *Captain Scarlet* was made the Century 21 Organisation was active not only in film production but also through its subsidiaries in records, toys, merchandising and publishing. The publishing company used Captain Scarlet in their comic *TV21* and he also appeared in many fan annuals.

The writers of this piece have obviously researched not only the television series but also the published spin-off material. As a result the book doesn't deal with the television series alone. It is a compilation of all the Captain Scarlet material produced in the sixties. I suspect the writers have also used some of their own ideas to link their researched material. The result is a very informative document which contains far more information than one could possibly glean from just the television screen.

If you enjoyed *Captain Scarlet*, or indeed any of my shows, then I am sure you will relish this unusual in-depth study.

Spectrum Is Green.

THE FINGER IS ON THE TRIGGER

Tricolour: Captains Scarlet, Ochre and Blue unwind in the Cloudbase lounge.

Courageous, determined, indestructible. The man they call Captain Scarlet!

Fear rules the twenty-first Century! The Mysterons of the planet Mars have declared war on Earth. Cold as silicon, merciless as an electric shock, the Mysterons have conquered death itself. They can create an exact copy of a human being and turn him against his family and friends. Bullets can't stop him and bombs will only slow him down, because Mysteron agents are indestructible.

Only one man can defeat the Mysterons. One man with the strength to fight off the Mysteron influence and regain control of his body. Captain Scarlet is that man – loyal to Earth but now completely indestructible. Brave as any hero that ever lived, Captain Scarlet has one big advantage; when his luck runs out, he can repair his wounds and return from the dead.

Captain Scarlet is the creation of Gerry Anderson, the man who gave *Stingray* and *Thunderbirds* to a worldwide TV audience. Captain Scarlet is radically different from any other puppet-hero Gerry Anderson produced in the 1960s, not least because he was born out of what seemed like disaster.

For Gerry Anderson, *Captain Scarlet and the Mysterons* began one morning in 1966 when ATV's Lew Grade told him that he didn't want another series of *Thunderbirds*. In the years since ATV had bought Anderson's struggling AP Films company, they'd produced *Supercar*, *Fireball XL5* and *Stingray*. *Thunderbirds* had been the biggest hit of all. Under the new name of *Century 21*, Anderson's company was creating comics, records and toys based on *Thunderbirds*. United

Artists had financed a movie called *Thunderbirds Are Go!* Lew Grade had even commissioned a further six episodes of the *Thunderbirds* TV series. So it was even more amazing, that late summer morning in 1966, when Grade decided that he wanted a totally new TV series. Even today, Anderson sounds surprised: 'because of the merchandising and because of the huge success, I wrongly assumed that he would continue with *Thunderbirds*. And he didn't.'

One thing was certain: Lew Grade was nobody's fool. In the ten years since Independent Television had begun in Britain, Grade had turned Associated Television into ITV's biggest money-maker. ATV ran stations in London and Birmingham, but most of the money was made by selling film series to America through ATV's Independent Television Corporation. As Gerry Anderson explains, 'These programmes were very expensive to make. To get that money back you'd have to sell to 80 countries individually, but if you take that total amount of world sales, 60 per cent of that global sum came from the States.' Even in America, the bullseye for which Grade aimed was the network sale. In one deal, Grade could sell *Fireball XL5* to the National Broadcasting Company, and the show would go out to hundreds of 'affiliated' stations across America. If a series didn't sell to the networks, the only alternative was to try and sell the show to each of the individual stations, one by one.

Thunderbirds was a massive success in Britain, but it did not get a network sale in America. To Lew Grade it must have been sense to forget *Thunderbirds* and channel the money into something new and better that he could sell to the American networks.

One of the biggest obstacles for *Thunderbirds* in America had been the lack of hour-long time slots. Consequently Gerry Anderson knew that his next show had to be fast, exciting and only half-an-hour long. As he drew up the pilot script

– the blue-print for the series – Anderson was aware that the puppets were better than ever. Mary Turner and 'Plugg' Shutt had built string-less puppets which could be controlled from the waist up, while John Read and Reg Hill had struggled tirelessly to reduce the size of the mouth control mechanism. With the smaller device lodged in the chest rather than the head, the size of the heads could be cut down so that they were in proportion with the bodies. Inspired both by the less-caricatured puppets and the success of Cliff Richard Junior in *Thunderbirds Are Go!*, Anderson saw a chance to get Hollywood 'guest-stars' for his new show. As he explained in the pilot script, an actor such as Dick Bogarde or Efrem Zimbalist Junior (then starring in *The FBI*) would lay down a voice track in the recording studio and then, 'a replica of his face would be made to appear in the film as a puppet.' The pilot script offers the example of *Dangerman*'s Patrick McGoohan playing the part of the World President. Unfortunately, time and money meant that the 'guest-puppet' idea had to be scrapped, but the concept of character-based storylines had already worked through into the pilot script.

In fact, Gerry Anderson was still so excited about his improved, life-like puppets that he dubbed Captain Scarlet, 'the Mechanical Man'. In the development script, the Mysterons kill the real Captain Scarlet and create an exact copy. This 'booby-trap' is captured at the end of the story and Spectrum's Doctor Fawn concludes that, 'with a specially designed computer it would be possible to bring him under our control.' The closing titles of the show would have underlined the 'mechanical' nature of Captain Scarlet by showing pictures of him in 'association with computers, printed circuits and electrodes'. Somewhere along the line, however, Gerry Anderson realised that viewers might find it hard to sympathise with what was basically a robot. Gradually, Captain Scarlet regained his flesh and soul and became the Indestructible Man.

Gerry Anderson had another reason for playing down the mechanical man angle. He'd realised that his puppets weren't quite as lifelike as he'd thought. 'Suddenly, all the movements had to be as realistic as the puppets and that made it difficult for the puppeteers to animate them.' Chief Puppeteer Christine Glanville explains that, 'when you see a puppet walk on film, the camera is so exacting that it exaggerates every movement, and they look as if they're skating!' Rather than show Captain Scarlet walking, the directors often used moving shots from the puppets' point of view, or even cut to another character as the puppets' footsteps were heard.

One landmark for the series was that Lieutenant Green and Melody Angel were the first black characters to star in an ITC series. This was a deliberate move on Gerry Anderson's part. 'When I made *Supercar* for ATV, we put quite a number of black characters in an episode because the story demanded it. ATV had an American advisor at that time, and he made us take out every black character and replace them with white characters and white voices. He said he would not be able to sell it to stations in the South because of the black characters. By the time *Captain Scarlet* came along, we had got to the point where American distributors were now prepared to accept black actors. I was always very anxious to promote racial harmony, so as soon as people had become more sensible I took advantage of it.'

As filming began, Anderson turned his attention to the merchandising. 'I knew only too well that if our shows didn't make a profit that would be the end of the studio and the end of me as a producer. Now the merchandise was extremely important, not only because it made a lot of money in its own right. A show creates a strong desire for a child to buy the toys, and when they get the toys and play with them, that in turn creates a desire to see the films again.' Keith Shackleton, the head of Century 21 Merchandising, had bounced back from the loss of *Thunderbirds* by spearheading the biggest TV-tie-in Britain had ever seen. Toys, sweets, and even clothes were busily being blazoned with the Spectrum symbol or Captain Scarlet's face. Aware of the success of Pye Records' *Thunderbirds* mini-albums, Gerry Anderson even assembled a pop group called The Spectrum to sing the *Captain Scarlet* theme over the end-titles. As Gerry himself admits, 'it soon became clear that they weren't going to be the next Beatles,' although the drummer, Keith Forsey, did go on to a successful career as a producer for performers like Billy Idol and such films as

Captain Scarlet and Dr. Kurnitz en route to Clondbase, secure within Spectrum's disguised VIP Transporter.

The Breakfast Club (he even wrote the Simple Minds hit, 'Don't You Forget About Me').

Century 21 also published its own range of comics, which generated pre-publicity for each new Anderson series. *TV Century 21* had given Lady Penelope her own picture strip months before *Thunderbirds* hit the TV screens, because the head of Century 21 Publications was Alan Fennell, who had written almost half the episodes of *Fireball XL5*, *Stingray* and *Thunderbirds*. Unfortunately, the success of *Thunderbirds* had helped to weaken the links between the comics and the studio. Century 21 now published *Lady Penelope*, *Candy* and *Solo* (starring *The Man from UNCLE*) in addition to *TV21* and a score of annuals and paperbacks. Fennell didn't have time to write episodes for *Captain Scarlet*, while Anderson's increased workload forced him to turn over his seat on the Century 21 Publishing board to Louis Benjamin of Pye Records.

The result was that Alan Fennell was almost as bewildered as his readers when the time came to create pre-publicity for *Captain Scarlet*. The format of the series was still being revised during filming, and the background to the series was quite complex. Fennell also found Scarlet himself quite perplexing: 'What works in film doesn't always work in comics. An indestructible hero presents problems in comics because there is nothing that can threaten him and therefore there is no drama.' The writers of *Superman* had been able to introduce Kryptonite to weaken their hero, but for *TV21* the format of *Captain Scarlet* was unalterable.

Months before the series had even finished filming, Fennell and his team got together around a table to create a background for *Captain Scarlet*. Starting with the most human characters, they introduced a strip called *The Angels* on the back page of *Lady Penelope*. Drawn by Jon Davis, the story began with five women pilots being called to a lonely Italian airfield and offered the chance to pilot unmarked white interceptors for an unseen master. Readers were soon curious to know the identity of the 'voice from the loud-speaker' which gave the Angels their orders, but one reader discovered the answer by a strange twist of fate. On Saturday 29 April 1967, Milton Finesilver was watching a comedy show which had been slotted into the end of BBC 1's transmission

Scarlet Lady: Rhapsody Angel first appeared in the *Lady Penelope* comic, but kept the truth about Spectrum under her hat.

after it had won the Golden Rose of Montreux. 'After it finished, I was flicking around the channels, even though the scheduled programmes had finished, and there on ATV London was the first episode of *Captain Scarlet*.' This was long before the advent of all-night television, so it is likely that Milton had stumbled upon an engineer's transmission test. Yet by another quirk of fate, Milton had already applied for a job at Century 21 Publications, and managed to astound office manager Tod Sullivan at his interview by relating details of a programme that only the upper rank of insiders were supposed to have seen.

By this time, Century 21 was blazing a trail for *Captain Scarlet* in almost all of the comics. *Solo* printed articles credited to Alan Fennell in which he warned of a malevolent force using strange powers to cause disasters across the globe. The force was eventually tracked down to the Mysterons, and *Solo* began running a feature called 'Spectrum News' ('so called because we believe the Mysterons cannot see colour'). Because the Mysterons were at the very heart of the new series, it would have been difficult to release much information about them without spoiling the surprises in *Captain Scarlet*'s first episode. For this reason, *Solo* began running a strip called 'The Mark of the Mysterons'. Drawn by ex-*Dan Dare* artist Don Harley, it was set in 1967, and followed *Solo* reporter John Marsh as he tried to warn a disbelieving world that alien bodysnatchers were invading Earth.

Over on the newspaper-style front page of *TV21*, Captain Black's Martian Excursion Vehicle was reported missing as it tried to trace the source of enigmatic radio signals in the Rock Snake Hills of Mars. As the editor of *TV21* asked which secret organisation had sent Captain Black to Mars, he had little idea just how lucky Black had been. Christine Glanville recalls that, as the first Mysteron victim, Captain Black was originally supposed to die at the end of the pilot episode. As a human, Captain Black looked quite bland, 'but once I'd painted him up to look gaunt and pallid, Gerry took one look and decided to keep him on as a regular.'

Back in *TV21*, a strip drawn by *Modesty Blaise* artist John Burns showed two journalists investigating a mysterious UFO hovering over Nice. The UFO was Cloudbase, speeding to intercept

Once a top Spectrum agent, Captain Black now obeys new masters.

Captain Black's Zero X ship on its return from Mars. In a stunning cliffhanger, the journalists flew directly into Captain Black's re-entry path, and although they avoided a collision, Captain Black was able to escape from Spectrum in the confusion. In the pages of *Lady Penelope*, Lieutenant Green was revealed as the voice behind the loudspeaker and the Angels were admitted into Spectrum. In the same week, the final issue of *Solo* climaxed with the first instalment of a comic strip about the history of the Mysterons. The story would continue in another comic.

On Friday 29th September, *Captain Scarlet and the Mysterons* premiered on ATV Midlands, closely followed by ATV London and Scottish

TV on Sunday 1st October. It would take a few weeks for the series to appear on the rest of the ITV stations, but until that time, the eager public could feast their eyes on the first part of *TV21*'s new *Captain Scarlet* strip. For the first time a Spectrum Pursuit Vehicle was seen charging across the landscape as Captain Scarlet raced to keep an appointment with destruction. In every home across the country, eager fingers flicked the TV switch to ITV. As the sky grew dark, anxious eyes fastened on shimmering blue screen, waiting for Captain Scarlet to take his first fateful walk down that mean dark alley.

**'I'll string along with you':
Captain Blue tends to a
wounded Symphony Angel.
A romance between the two
characters bubbled
sedately beneath the
surface.**

ONE MAN FATE HAS MADE INDESTRUCTIBLE

Captain Scarlet is like no Supermarionation hero that has gone before. Scott Tracy and Troy Tempest are both brave and intelligent but the success of their missions depends on the superior technology of the machines they pilot. Captain Scarlet succeeds, not because of his Spectrum Pursuit Vehicle or Spectrum Passenger Jet, but because the Mysterons have made him indestructible. Yet even before he joined Spectrum, Captain Scarlet was unique. Under his real name of Paul Metcalfe, he was the youngest Colonel in the World Army Air Force, trained to pilot a variety of aircraft and expert with hundreds of weapons, from the latest Ultrasonic Bazooka to the ancient Bundi dagger. Drilled to survive in the toughest of conditions, Metcalfe demonstrated a mental resilience which coupled with his humour and concern for others made him a prime candidate for Spectrum.

Under his codename of Captain Scarlet, Paul Metcalfe is Spectrum's top agent. In 'The Launching', Colonel White obviously feels that Scarlet can be the most diplomatic of the Captains, as he is sent to convince America's President Roberts of the danger of the Mysteron threat. However, 'Lunarville 7' shows that Scarlet's single-mindedness can sometimes override his subtlety, when he makes it very clear to the Lunar Controller's assistant that he is interested in the mysterious Humboldt Sea.

In 'White As Snow', and 'Treble Cross', Colonel White offers Scarlet the chance to command Spectrum in his absence. In Colonel White's eyes, Scarlet has only one great failing,

underlined in 'Flight to Atlantica' when he says, 'As usual, Captain, you were too impetuous.' Evidence for White's assessment is seen in 'Treble Cross' when he pre-empts the Colonel's order and announces that he and Blue will fly to Slaton air base, while in 'White As Snow' he is openly critical of White's decision to destroy the incoming satellite and makes no attempt to disguise his distaste. However, he is prepared to admit that he was wrong and risks his career in order to make amends. But whatever his personality may be it was the Mysterons who changed Captain Scarlet

Captain Scarlet may be wounded, but even as the SPJ ejector seat floats to earth, his body is rapidly repairing itself.

From behind his computerised desk, Colonel White briefs his two top agents.

and inadvertently made him more than human; a weapon every bit as powerful as the Thunderbird machines or Stingray!

The origin and powers of the Mysterons are still unknown. The first Captain Scarlet annual, written while the series was in production, speculates that the Mysterons were actually a 'strange race of people from an unknown galaxy' who landed upon Mars, and settled there, with computers 'planning constructing and running their city for them'. The annual continues to speculate that the Mysterons eventually tired of Mars and took off again in their spaceships, leaving their city of computers behind them. This intriguing scenario is slightly contradicted by *The Mysterons*, a comic strip published in *TV Tornado* from September 1967 onwards. To make the job of the

Red planet Mars: home of the Mysteron menace.

illustrator easier, the comic strip implies that the Mysterons are actually formless beings controlled by a giant computer, who rapidly take on their 'ancient, Mysteron shape' when exposed to alien atmospheres and environments.

These two contrasting theories highlight the fact that no one was completely certain what the Mysterons were. However, the evidence of the TV series suggests that intelligences on Mars were actually called the Mysterons. The pilot episode opens on a Martian Excursion Vehicle crewed by World Space Patrol officers under the command of Spectrum's Captain Black. His mission is to find the source of strange radio signals detected on Earth, and in an ancient valley it is revealed: a shimmering, opalescent city which glows against the rocks like a giant pinball machine. Inside the

Mysteron moonbase: built by robots, it showed no signs of life.

city, lights pulsate behind the walls as a sleek, piston-like device pumps rhythmically up and down. A deep, unearthly voice echoes around the complex: 'The first of the Earth travellers have arrived. Like us they have a curiosity about the Universe in which we live. We must take a closer look at them.'

If the Mysterons purposely transmitted the signals in order to lure intelligent life to Mars, they obviously underestimated man's capacity for trust. As the Mysterons take that 'closer look' at the MEV, the crew mistake the panning cameras for weapons and assume that they're about to be attacked. Captain Black gives the order to open fire, and whether through an extremely destructive missile, or a direct hit on a power source, the city is turned into a wasteland within seconds.

As the dust clears, an automatic device grinds into action, shining a glittering green light over the wreckage. Before the eyes of the astonished Earthmen, the complex re-materialises. The Mysteron voice vows revenge for this act of aggression and announces that one of the MEV crew will become their agent. The cameras close in on Captain Black, his eyes now dark and lifeless.

This opening sequence suggests that the Mysterons cannot or will not move outside their city. Although the Mysterons employ robot vehicles to build and defend their moonbase in 'Lunarville 7' and 'Crater 101', the pre-programmed vehicles are easily outwitted by electronics genius Lieutenant Green. Since the completed Mysteron moonbase shows no signs of intelligence this raises the question of why the Mysterons should physically build a city on the Moon when they had already taken control of Lunarville 7. The Mysteron complex displays a number of features (such as an hypnotic screen and an anti-gravity shaft) designed for humans plus a power source which is easily identified and removed. This suggests that the entire moonbase was just a giant 'rat trap' designed to test the intelligence and ingenuity of the Spectrum personnel.

The answers are never revealed in the TV series, but it seems most likely that the Mysterons are a form of Artificial Intelligence which has evolved into something more than mechanical yet less than human. This would explain the apparent petulance of their decision to exterminate an entire race in return for an attack by three men.

Blue and Green watch Captain Scarlet remove the power source of the Mysteron's lunar complex.

As for the powers of the Mysterons, these are graphically demonstrated in the pilot episode as Captain Brown and Captain Scarlet speed to the defence of the World President. The Mysterons can transmit raw energy across space, using this energy to manipulate the timing mechanism of a nuclear bomb, take control of a speeding lorry or, in the pilot episode, blow out the tyre of Scarlet and Brown's saloon car.

In the crash which follows, the two green haloes which will become the Mysteron signature drift across the bloodied bodies of Captains Brown and Scarlet. Just as the beam of light from a photocopier passes over a picture, registering the different light and dark areas of the image, so the Mysteron scanners probe deep into the microscopic structure of the two men. Every twist and turn of their molecular structure is transmitted back to Mars and translated into the bio-mechanical code of the Mysterons. Just as computers can add colour to black and white movies, or reconstruct photographs that have been blemished by age, the Mysterons can piece together the molecular structure of people and objects, even if they have been destroyed.

In less time than it takes to blink an eye, the Mysterons have changed the molecular structure of Scarlet and Brown, and transmitted the information back to Earth. Just as a photocopier needs paper and ink to print out an image, the Mysterons use the raw energy they can transmit to create duplicates of Scarlet and Brown.

These doppelgangers are identical in appearance to Scarlet and Brown, and like spies who have learned the life-story of a close friend, they can imitate the original exactly. However, their minds are activated by a Mysteron control signal, carrying operating instructions for the body and a fanatical devotion to the cause of the Mysterons. This control signal also enables the fake Scarlet to decode the extra-sensory communications signal radiated by his fellow Mysterons, making it possible for Scarlet to receive instructions from Captain Black many miles away.

When the Mysterons create a duplicate, they give him, her or it the power of retro-metabolism. All living beings have the power to grow new skin or mend broken bones over a period of time, but Mysteron duplicates can quickly repair any damage or wounds, even ones which would be fatal in a human. The energy needed to repair the wounds is collected through the skin of the Mysteron and stored within its cells in much the same way that a plant collects the energy from sunlight and converts it into a more useful form. Unlike a plant, the Mysteron doppelgangers can release this stored energy in a single violent burst, as Captain Brown demonstrates when he literally explodes beside the World President. In the pilot episode, Colonel White assumes that Brown was carrying a bomb, but by 'Point 783' Spectrum have deduced that the Mysterons can literally self-destruct.

The duplicate Captain Scarlet manages to kidnap the World President just before the body of the original Captain Scarlet is discovered. This untidy habit of leaving bodies and wreckage

Every move you make: Captain Black co-ordinates another mission for his Mysteron masters.

behind becomes such an Achilles' heel for the Mysterons that it is easy to suspect that the Mysterons are simply playing with the Earthmen by leaving clues behind. Yet the fact that Captain Scarlet's body is found so quickly also underlines the question of what happened to Captain Black's earthly remains.

Captain Black was taken over by the Mysterons as he sat in the control cabin of the MEV. Yet Black was not apparently duplicated. Subsequent episodes reveal that he stayed with the Zero X ship until it reached Earth. The next time he is seen in the pilot episode, Black is pallid and unshaven and his American accent has been replaced by the uninflected tones of the Mysterons. Could Captain Black still be alive under Mysteron control? Certainly, when Lieutenant Dean suggests a quick escape after destroying the Mysteron City, the real Captain Black insists that they go down and survey the ruins. Wouldn't it be a monumental punishment for someone with such assurance and self-control to be conscious but unable to stop his body from carrying out the misdeeds of the Mysterons?

It seems clear, in episodes such as 'Fire at Rig 15', that Black's body has been altered in some way; he acts as a conduit for the ultrasonic rays which knock out Jason Smith, and also displays a phosphorescent effect when the lights are turned out. Yet in most episodes, Captain Black is simply carrying out the assassinations which create new Mysteron slaves (usually by shooting or causing car accidents) and then 'relaying the instructions of the Mysterons'. Significantly, though, Black never puts himself in physical danger. On the rare occasions when he is about to be captured, ('Model Spy' and 'Heart of New York') the Mysterons simply teleport him and his automobile out of the scene. Could it be that Captain Black, alone among the Mysteron agents, is not indestructible? Perhaps the reason that no body was found in the MEV is that this is still the original Captain Black.

In theory then, all Mysterons are indestructible. So why do they always die when their missions fail? The explanation seems to be that the Mysterons shut off their control signal. If the duplicate is of a car or helicopter, it simply rolls to a halt or crashes. Subsequent episodes establish that electricity is the only sure way to kill a

Mysteron. 'Flight 104' shows Scarlet and Blue gaining control of a Mysteron-controlled jet when an electric power station cuts off the control signal from Mars. Of course, an electric pulse can damage a Mysteron just as it would (fatally) damage a human, but electricity will also block the control signal of the Mysteron. The importance of Spectrum's Electron Gun, therefore, lies not in its capacity to kill a Mysteron, but in its ability to prevent the dead Mysteron from being regenerated. Without the control signal, the Mysteron dies, unable to activate its fantastic powers of retro-metabolism. So it seems that, if a duplicate fails in its mission, its Mysteron masters simply abandon it. They turn off the control signal and leave it to die.

Yet Captain Scarlet was different. As he failed in his mission and fell 800 feet from the Car-Vu Tower, the Mysterons cut his control signal. Any other duplicate would have fallen to the ground and been instantly killed. Captain Scarlet did not, and the reason for this seems to lie in an oversight by the Mysterons.

Can electricity kill a Mysteron? Spectrum's Intelligence Agency devised this electron gun in *Spectrum Strikes Back* but for the rest of the series, bullets worked just as well.

Black's cat: Mysteronised fashion model Helga is a perfect duplicate of the original. Even during a kidnap she keeps her best side to the camera.

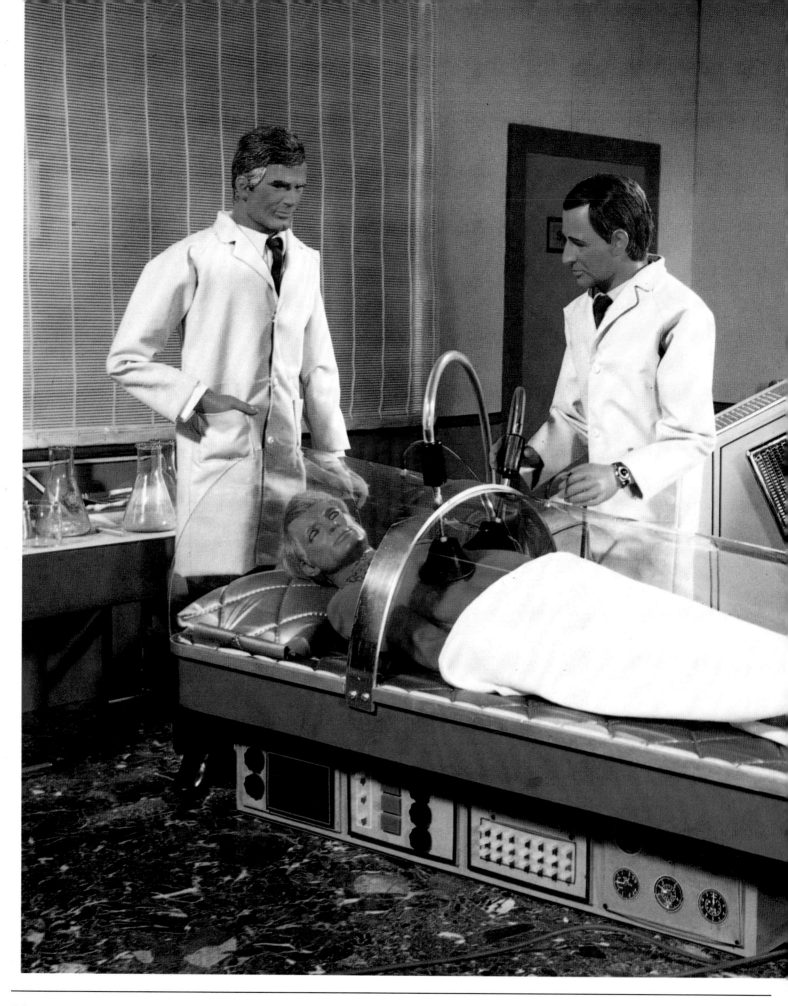

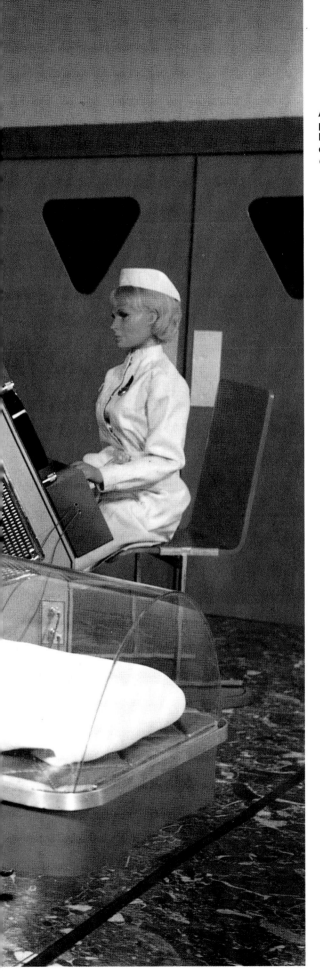

A resuscitation machine preserves a fragment of Major Gravener's consciousness in *Treble Cross*.

The 'Treble Cross' episode demonstrates that it is not necessary for the human to be dead when he is scanned by the Mysterons. (Although Major Gravener is comatose, and referred to as 'dead' in the episode, it is obvious that he has not actually died. Even a few seconds without oxygen will damage the human brain forever, but there are several recorded instances of people who 'drowned', like Major Gravener, but were saved by the Mammalian Diving Response, which automatically slows down the heartbeat and channels oxygen to the brain. One woman even recovered in a mortuary after having been pronounced 'dead' on the slab.)

What the Mysterons need is a person who is unconscious and unable to think. Captain Scarlet illustrates the problems the Mysterons face when they do duplicate someone who is not dead or unconscious. As Scarlet tells Doctor Fawn in 'Winged Assassin', his final memories after the car crash are of the flames closing in on his body as he lay beside the wreckage. To be precise, those are the final memories of the original Captain Scarlet. As the Mysterons scanned his body, Scarlet was still struggling to survive, deep within the recesses of his mind. Because his mind was still active, that struggle was part of the information copied by the Mysterons. Although they altered the physical structure of the new Captain Scarlet, they failed to notice that the original mind was being copied along with the memories and personality. Just as computers can create a default program which takes over the machine when no other program is running, so Scarlet's mind lay dormant within the brain of the Mysteron doppelganger, waiting to be awoken.

As the duplicate lay shattered on the ground after the fall from the Car-Vu, the real Captain Scarlet's will took over where it had left off, desperately trying to survive and activating the regenerative powers of its strange new body.

Captain Scarlet is indestructible, but this does not make him a superman. It's not surprising that he still sounds uncertain as he and Blue debate ramming the wheels of a speeding jet with the SPV (Spectrum Pursuit Vehicle), in 'Winged Assassin'. 'That'd be suicide!' rasps Blue. 'For you, yes,' says Scarlet, 'For me . . .?' Still only half convinced of his powers, he pulls the switch which will eject Blue from the SPV. It's a measure of his bravery that Scarlet is willing to gamble his life on the basis of one diagnosis from Doctor Fawn. Even when he knows that he is indestructible, he is not immune to pain and feels every cut, graze and bullet wound. Of course, even though it seems likely that electricity would not kill Captain Scarlet (because he does not need the Mysteron control signal to keep him alive) he is understandably wary of putting this theory to the test. In 'Noose of Ice', when told that the Eskimo Booster station churns out 100,000 volts, Scarlet muses 'dangerously high'. He does, none the less, chase the Mysteron saboteur into the Booster station, thus 'endangering' himself.

Despite the gifts that the Mysterons have inadvertently given him, Captain Scarlet is still the hero because of the way he uses those gifts. Each episode of the series reveals a little more about the physiology of the Mysterons. Scarlet's body can hold energy in reserve for mending wounds, so it comes as little surprise that he also needs very little sleep, prowling the night-time corridors in 'Lunarville 7', 'Inferno' and 'Shadow of Fear'.

More perplexing is the Mysteron reaction to X-rays revealed in 'Operation Time'. Obviously the process referred to as 'X-raying' is far in advance of even today's science because in 'Spectrum Strikes Back' this 'X-ray Camera' is used in much the same way as a conventional Polaroid (to take an X-ray picture, the subject must be placed between the film and the radiation source since the X-rays have to pass through the subject). It appears that the 'X-ray machines' are actually an improvement on today's process of Nuclear Magnetic Resonance, which causes the molecules of the body to emit radiation.

Like a walking solar battery, Captain Scarlet is constantly recharging himself from the sun's rays, ready for his next duel with death.

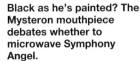

Black as he's painted? The Mysteron mouthpiece debates whether to microwave Symphony Angel.

Whatever the physics behind it, this 'X-ray machine' is used to take pictures of a human skull prior to brain surgery. When a Mysteron accidentally places his hand on the patient, some side-effect of the retro-metabolic process causes the picture of his hand to gradually turn positive. In 'Spectrum Strikes Back', a Mysteron Detector is developed which takes an 'X-ray' picture of humans and a positive picture of Mysterons – including Captain Scarlet. Bizarre as it may sound, Captain Scarlet is also able to 'fog' a conventional camera in 'Flight 104', even though Captain Black is photographed without any strange side-effects in 'Manhunt'.

Disassociated from Mysteron control, Captain Scarlet is now unable to decipher the radiation from other Mysterons. Just as an ordinary phone receiver will pick up an unintelligible squawk from a Fax machine, the physical effect of the Mysteron radiation confuses Scarlet's body, creating a sensation similar to car sickness. It appears that some Mysterons are able to retune the frequency of their personal radiation, since Scarlet's 'sixth sense' doesn't always warn him of a Mysteron presence. Strangely though, Captain

Black appears unwilling to face Captain Scarlet, talking to him from behind a closed door in 'Special Assignment'.

It is noticeable that, although Captain Black often assassinates on the orders of the Mysterons, he refrains from killing when it is not entirely necessary. In 'Big Ben Strikes Again', for instance, he knocks out Macey, the driver of the nuclear transporter, even though this means the man is soon at large and able to give Spectrum a valuable lead. An apparently sensitive aspect of his nature is shown in the episode 'Manhunt' when, having forced Symphony Angel into a radiation chamber, he apologises for what he has to do and assures her that the radiation will kill her within three minutes. Having set the process in motion, he seems uneasy as he watches the girl weaken, and turns the machine on to maximum output, as if to speed up the process. A few moments later, he shuts the machine off, explaining that 'Mysterons also have compassion'. An interesting revelation and, unless Black is trying to cover for some surviving human trait, a strong indication that the Mysterons are anything but the cold and pernicious minds they seem to be.

SPECTRUM IS GREEN

Colonel White briefs Spectrum's elite of colour-coded officers in the Cloudbase conference room.

Cloudbase: Spectrum's solitary sentinel of the stratosphere.

Captain Scarlet may be Spectrum's top agent, but just what is Spectrum and why was it formed? The name of Spectrum was chosen to signify the fact that its agents are not limited to one area of operation (such as the sea or space) but instead cover the entire range of World Security just as the light spectrum spans the complete range of colours.

Spectrum answers only to the World President, James Younger, who is the head of the World Government. Although the nations of 21st-century Earth still have their own national leaders such as President Roberts of America, they are united by the World Senate, which sits at Unity City. Spanning the coral reefs of Bermuda, Unity City is a fusion-powered zone of such complexity that it is dubbed 'Futura City' by the locals.

Yet the world is not at peace. To the East of Europe lies Bereznik, a small but predatory state whose battalions of robot tanks present a constant menace to its neighbours. Below the pacific Ocean, Titan and his Aquaphibian hordes continue to threaten the surface world.

To combat these threats, the World Government has established Supreme Headquarters Earth Forces, which from its New York base controls four unique defence agencies around the globe. The World Navy and World Aquanaut Security Patrol protect the oceans, while the World Army Air Force co-ordinates the air and land defences of member nations.

The World Space Patrol is responsible for the defence and exploration of Earth's borders, and controls several specialised divisions. The XK Fleet provides a shuttle service to the commercial Moonbases, while for longer journeys the WSP turns to its nuclear-powered Zero-X craft which have the extensive life-support systems needed for long-distance missions. The WSP also maintains the XL squadron based at Space City Atoll in the Pacific. Because the faster-than-light engines of the XL ships are extremely expensive to operate the ships are mainly used for emergencies and journeys to the edge of Earth's solar system, beyond the range of virtually all XK and Zero-X ships.

Unfortunately, these agencies, together with the World Police Corps and Universal Secret Service, were and are hampered by legal and diplomatic regulations. At a meeting of the World Security Council in January 2065, the Supreme Commander of Earth Forces put forward the idea of a new organisation. Capable of swift intelligence gathering and even faster reaction, the un-named agency would have full police powers, both on Earth and in space. As the World President began preparing the authorisation for this unnamed organisation, a committee was appointed to bring it to life. Working from an empty office above the Dewar-Elf shopping mall in Unity City, the seven men and women, whose identities are hidden to this day, spent months on end sifting through personnel files to locate the ideal candidates.

By the autumn of 2065, the committee had selected Charles Gray, a former admiral in the World Navy, as leader of the new organisation. Working from plans drawn up by a civilian

Codename Casa Blanca: built in the style of Thomas Jefferson from radiation-proof materials, the US President's home rests in the grounds of the Pentagon.

engineering genius, the committee used several anonymous 'shell' companies to commission the individual components of Cloudbase, the unique floating headquarters of the new agency. The finished parts were then secretly shuttled out to an abandoned Weather Satellite where engineers from the WSP and WAAF were waiting to assemble the pre-fabricated sections. Supervising the construction was Conrad Turner, a WSP Colonel who had been one of the unnamed organisation's first recruits – and one of their best. Working in the zero gravity of space, Turner pushed his crew to finish Cloudbase in record time. All that was needed now was to move Cloudbase down into Earth's atmosphere.

As Colonel Turner triggered the chemical rockets Cloudbase blasted free from the weather satellite. The forces of gravity quickly began to rattle and shake the massive structure as it plummeted towards the Pacific Ocean. Finally, the hurricane force of the Hover Combine engines began to slow Cloudbase's fall until it stabilised at forty thousand feet.

During 2066 Cloudbase was equipped, the prototype Angel Interceptors were delivered, and the five women pilots chosen to fly them were selected and trained. By the summer of 2067, Spectrum was fully manned, fully equipped and ready to roll. Finally, after long negotiations with his fellow politicians, the World President was able to sign the Charter which gave Spectrum official recognition.

Most of Spectrum's agents work, undercover, at the worldwide network of camouflaged Spectrum Ground Bases. Occasionally a Cloudbase officer will come to collect a Spectrum Pursuit Vehicle, and when the agent is satisfied with their identification, he or she will push the button which unveils the SPV. Whether hidden behind the sliding wall of a casino, or inside an oil storage tank, the SPV is soon hurtling into action.

Developed from the Zeus Combat Tank, the SPV is Spectrum's most remarkable and vital piece of land-based hardware. For use in cases of extreme emergency, the SPV provides Spectrum agents with a fast and virtually unstoppable means of transport. With its roof-mounted dorsal-fin and sleek, streamlined body, the SPV resembles a bizarre, road-travelling shark. Armed to the teeth and with a top speed of 200 mph, it is a fearsome adversary; just like a Rottweiler never letting go of its prey.

Blue ribbon: Angel escort races SPV towards the danger zone!

Spectrum is environmentally friendly: even when converted to a jet-pack, the SPV power unit works on hydrogen and oxygen and produces no harmful emissions.

As its name and design imply, the SPV comes into its own when used in the pursuit of an otherwise unstoppable quarry. In 'Winged Assassin', for example, Captain Scarlet chases the Mysteronised DT19 Stratojet along the runway at London Airport, before ramming his SPV into the plane's undercarriage. A slower vehicle would have been unable to match the aircraft's speed; while anything less durable could not have withstood the incredible friction generated as it chafed against the jet's rapidly spinning tyres.

Another example of the SPV's structural strength can be seen in 'Point 783' when, during a clash with the Unitron Combat Tank, both vehicles plummet over the edge of a desert canyon, crashing on to the rocky ground hundreds of feet below. Considered by the army to be their ultimate weapon, the Unitron it totally destroyed by the impact, whilst the SPV remains virtually unscratched and undamaged.

Should a more conventional form of attack be required a powerful retractable cannon is housed beneath a sliding hatch, located in the nose of the vehicle. Capable of delivering explosive missiles with computer-guided accuracy, the awesome destructive power of this weapon can be seen during the closing moments of 'The Trap', when Captain Blue unleashes a volley of shots which completely destroy Glengarry Castle.

Access to the SPV is gained through two hermetically sealed hatches, which slide outwards and inwards on a telescopic ram. Once inside, the most incredible feature of the SPV's design becomes apparent. For extra safety during a crash, both the driver's and co-driver's seats face towards the rear of the vehicle; forward visibility is gained by means of a high-definition television monitor. This unique set-up is shown to have just one major drawback, when, in 'Codename Europa', a Mysteron agent causes an SPV to crash by disrupting the TV signal with an electronic jamming device. In an emergency both seats, fitted with rockets, can be ejected through the roof of the vehicle. Once a safe height has been achieved, in-built parachutes are deployed.

Situated in the floor, between the two seats, is a sliding hatch giving access to the SPV's portable hydrogenic power unit. As soon as the power pack is removed, the main six-wheel drive shuts down, and the four smaller wheels (powered by an emergency battery) take over. The driver then selects an option from the keyboard situated beside the steering console. Easily removed, the power unit can be adapted quickly into anything from a sea-sled to a power-drill. Whatever option is chosen, the on-board computer quickly delivers the components needed to adapt the power pack. The most frequently used option is the one-man jet-thruster pack, which is put to good use firstly by Captain Blue in 'The Mysterons' and then by Captain Scarlet in such episodes as 'The Trap' and 'Expo 2068'. It should be noted that each SPV carries five different helmets corresponding to the colours of the five Spectrum Cap-

tains. Since the on-board computer demands an identification code from the officer who keys in a selection, it is immediately able to deliver a Scarlet helmet to Captain Scarlet or a Blue helmet to Captain Blue.

One intriguing feature of the SPV was the set of rear-mounted caterpillar tracks which, according to the 1967 annual, allowed it to climb mountains by tilting back into a vertical position. Anyone sitting inside would have literally hung from their rear facing seat if this manoeuvre had been attempted, and Derek Meddings, who designed the SPV, has recently confirmed that the tracks were intended to flip down for extra traction.

Piloted by Melody Angel, a Spectrum helicopter tracks a Mysteron agent across the Himalaya.

Whether inside or outside the SPV, each Spectrum officer is in constant contact with Cloudbase through the personal computer stored in the epaulettes of his or her uniform. If the officer receives a message from Colonel White, the epaulettes flash on and off, at the same time emitting an infra-red beam which activates the microphone and speakers situated in the officer's cap. The other standard item of equipment is the Spectrum blaster, carried in the waist holster. This Combustion Augmented Plasma gun carries a magazine of sixteen shots. Each cartridge is packed with liquid propellant and is fired by an electronic pulse from the battery in the handle.

If the Spectrum agent is out of bullets and his SPV has crashed, he can still call upon the Spectrum Auxiliary. From Maximum Security Centres such as Vandon Base, they can despatch a battalion of armed guards or Radar Tracking Vans manned by trained operators. The Spectrum Auxiliary also maintains a fleet of fast-moving vehicles for the use of Spectrum agents. To provide Spectrum agents with a fast, efficient means of transport for use during routine operations, Spectrum developed the unique, wedge-shaped Spectrum Saloon Car. Fitted with racing tyres and a roof-mounted stabilising fin, the cars are capable of speeds in excess of 150 miles per hour and incorporate a sturdy roll cage, the central rib of which runs the entire length of the car, dividing the windscreen and ending in a strengthened nose buffer, which can be used to ram enemy vehicles.

The five-seater Saloon Car is used frequently during the series, both as a patrol car and an

Spectrum saloon car: overhead shot highlights the liquid crystal windscreens which can turn opaque at the touch of a button.

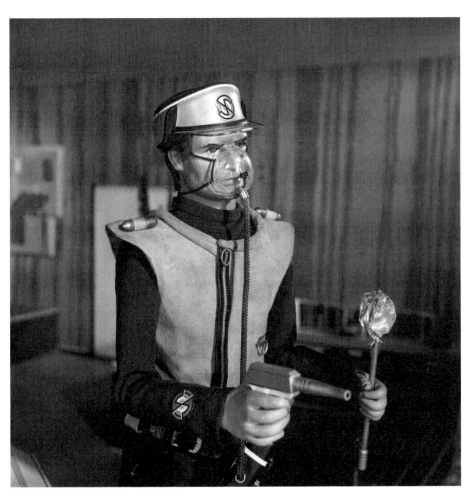

Under pressure: Captain Ochre grabs a respirator before blasting open one of the protective portholes in Cloudbase. Decompression could kill him before the bomb in his hand explodes!

integral part of any Spectrum roadblock or Motorcade. Easily identifiable, the car bears the distinctive Spectrum emblem on both doors and, like the Ferrari, is available exclusively in a startling shade of red.

When Spectrum has advance warning of an attack, however, they roll out the Maximum Security Vehicle. This grey, armadillo-shaped vehicle is pressurised with its own internal life-support system. Designed to survive the toughest assault, the MSV has bullet-proof twin tyres and a shell which sandwiches a radiation-damping alloy between a steel interior and an armour plate exterior. Although its portholes may appear to offer a tempting target for a Mysteron sniper, they are actually made from high-density boro-silicate which is impervious to both bullets and radiation.

Despite the strength of the MSV it is often used for decoy duties to draw attention away from the Very Important Personnel Carrier. Disguised as a petrol tanker, the VIPC is equipped with a luxurious, bomb-proof passenger cabin, Although this

passenger cabin is virtually indestructible, the truck section is not. Due to the hazardous nature of this assignment, the VIPC is usually driven by an experienced officer such as Captain Ochre.

Finally, from the roof-top hangars of the Maximum Security Centres, the Spectrum Auxiliary can launch their purpose-built helicopters. Although primarily used for transport, the Spectrum helicopter is equipped with a rapid-fire 20mm cannon at the front of the cockpit. The tough Maylon skids are capable of landing in any land or sea conditions, while the ring-shaped tail gives stability at speeds of up to 302 miles per hour. The tremendous power of its twin-turbo jets gives the Spectrum helicopter the lift it needs to reach Cloudbase.

Floating seven miles above sea level, Cloudbase is the nerve centre of Spectrum. It functions around the clock, with its crew of six hundred working constant four-hour shifts. To combat fatigue, Cloudbase employs the Room of Sleep, an hypnotic chamber with diffused lighting and 'weightless' gimbal-slung couches which make it possible for Cloudbase operatives to cram eight hours sleep into thirty minutes.

Being so close to the Sun, Cloudbase is ideally located for solar power. Most of Cloudbase's surface area is covered by non-reflective photovoltaic cells which capture the Sun's rays and convert them into electricity. This is directed to the twenty liquid Cahelium engines which power the four hover-combines. The combines keep Cloudbase afloat by sucking air in through the horizontal ducts and then circulating it at great pressure. The air is then blown out an an angle, creating a cushion of air upon which Cloudbase rests. Although this must seem an astounding achievement to 20th-century eyes, the combines are still not operating at their full capacity. Extra reserves of power can be called upon to generate horizontal jets. Working in conjunction with the fan-rudder located on the stern, these jets can move Cloudbase's position above the Earth.

Despite being inside the Earth's atmosphere, Cloudbase is built on similar principles to a space station, since it must operate within extremes of low temperature, low air pressure and high cosmic radiation. Cloudbase is pressurised and can only be entered through air locks. If a hole was knocked in the hull of Cloudbase, the air would

quickly rush out, carrying people and furniture with it. For this reason, most of the rooms in Cloudbase are windowless. Those areas which do contain windows, such as the rooftop promenade deck, employ a toughened glass which is also designed to filter out ultraviolet rays. In addition, face mask respirators are stored within recesses at regular intervals throughout the base. If Cloudbase should be damaged beyond repair, every crew member is within sixty seconds' sprinting distance of one of the many gyroscopic escape capsules which are clamped on to all the emergency exits.

Cloudbase is constantly patrolled by small, tracked robots which both clean and inspect every inch of its interior. Even the flight deck is regularly swabbed by the robots in order to remove potentially hazardous oil leaks and vented jet fuel. Signals from the robots are relayed back to the control centre, just behind the observation tubes in the bridge section.

The control room is entered through a green sliding door, beneath which is a moving walkway that leads directly to Colonel White's desk. Beside the walkway is Lieutenant Green's control console, a glass display screen at least fifteen feet long. All incoming information is assessed by the console before being passed to the Spectrum Information Centre for recording. A digest of this information can be read direct from the light pattern display or paper print-outs. Diagrams and video pictures can also be displayed on the colour liquid crystal display screen behind Colonel White's desk.

Mounted on a steam-powered rotating platform (steam is another cheap source of energy on Cloudbase due to direct solar heating of water pipes) Colonel White's desk is a compact supercomputer running a program tailored to White's own personality. In any one minute, the desk can assess the hundreds of reports being relayed by Lieutenant Green's communications console and highlight those of special interest to the Colonel. By pressing the appropriate coloured button on his desk, Colonel White can instantly contact the

View into Cloudbase control room, as Colonel White surveys the observation tube.

As Cloudbase reels from the Mysteron attack, Colonel White prepares to go down with his command.

corresponding Spectrum Captain anywhere in the world. Voice recognition circuits within the computer react to Colonel White's verbal commands by instantly withdrawing information stored at the Spectrum Information Centre and displaying it, either as a diagram or moving pictures, on the screen behind him.

Next door to the control room is the Spectrum Information Centre. Painted in warm pastel tones, this air-conditioned room is actually maintained at a constant chill to keep its complex of Seventh Generation computers from overheating. Although slower in operation than the control room computers, these 'super brains' are infinitely more powerful. Where most computers, however fast, can only work on the information they receive, the Seventh Generation computer is capable of intuitive thought based on incomplete information. Primitive in comparison to the Mysterons, these digital detectives are still a vital asset in Spectrum's attempts to outguess the enemy.

The far wall of the Spectrum Information Centre is a swirling, pulsating sea of colour – in fact, this wall-to-wall plastic shield contains the liquid plasma that is the physical store of verbal, digital and video reports transmitted by Spectrum ground stations.

Behind the Spectrum Information Centre is the Observation Room, a mass of telescanners, lasers, multi-spectral scanners and return-beam vidicons monitoring outer space and planet Earth. Radio altimeters keep a constant check on Cloudbase's height while the spectral irradiance monitor measures the intensity of solar radiation hitting Cloudbase. Information from the Observation Room is relayed back to Spectrum Information Centre and Lieutenant Green's control console.

Beneath the control deck is level C, which contains an Auxiliary Generator, the Circular Conference Room and the Sick Bay. The domain of Doctor Fawn is in effect a miniature hospital. Chemical analysers can perform complex blood tests within seconds, while the Auto-Pharmacist can synthesise anything from headache pills to a cure for snake-bites within fifteen minutes. Apart from the consulting room, the Sick Bay contains a fully equipped operating theatre, intensive care module, isolation ward and an electronics lab in which Doctor Fawn experiments on his development of robot surgeons.

Lieutenant Green controls Cloudbase and much of Spectrum from this one communications computer.

Below the bridge the two hollow support struts contain ventilated escalator units which carry Spectrum staff down into the flight deck. The escalators terminate inside the two nearest hover-combines, which are insulated against the tremendous noise of the engines. Here the staff must transfer to another of the moving walkways which criss-cross Cloudbase. At the far end of Deck E is the Amber Room, duty station for the Angels. Like the recreation room that is shared by both the Angels and Spectrum Captains, the Amber Room contains a mass of entertainment equipment which helps pass the hours in between alerts. As Spectrum's first line of defence, the five pilots work continuous four-hour shifts. Each Angel takes her turn as Angel leader, stationed permanently in Angel One, ready for immediate take-off. During change-overs, a red light flashes on Lieutenant Green's console if Angel One is unmanned for more than sixty seconds.

A launch alert automatically fires up the engines of Angel One, and the jet is hurled forward by a steam catapult running below the surface of the flight deck. Down below in the Amber Room, the two remaining Angels take their seats in the recessed elevator. The opaque glass shield slides shut forming a pressure seal, and the elevator rides up towards an airlock on the next level. At this point, a computerised switch-back takes over, moving the Angels sideways to positions beneath the two remaining aircraft (a third track leads forwards towards the position of Angel One, which is boarded by the same elevator). Here, they enter pressurised glass chutes which extend up through the flight deck and lock on to the entrance hatches located in the base of the Angel jets. As the air pressure within the chutes and jets is equalised, the pilots are raised up and locked into position within the cockpit. The chutes retract and the jet engines fire automatically as the catapults launch the Angels forward into space.

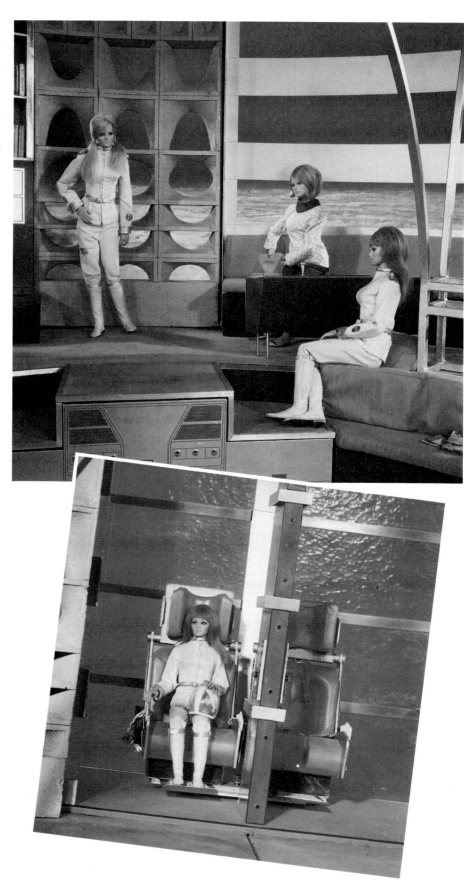

The Amber Room: Destiny, Symphony and Rhapsody Angels relax.

Rhapsody Angel in the elevator seat, ready to begin her four hours stand-by duty in Angel One.

Based on the World Army Air Force Viper Jet, the Angel interceptors are designed for super-sonic combat. The needle-sharp nose contains sophisticated proton navigation systems which are linked to the on-board computer. Flight information is projected on to a transparent green screen facing the pilot. Armed with a 9mm cannon and five Seraph missiles, the Angels fly on JP12 fuel, processed exclusively by Spectrum's refinery at Bensheba. Launched horizontally for speed, the Angels are also equipped with Vertical Take Off and Landing jets which are vital to the Cloudbase landing procedure.

Locking on to a microwave beam projected from Cloudbase, the Angel 'rides' the beam down towards the flight deck. At the rear of the deck is a magnetic 'trap' raised hydraulically into a vertical position (this should not be confused with the large directional fan at the other end of Cloudbase). Guided by her on-board computer, the pilot triggers her landing jets and steers towards the 'trap'. As the jet is magnetically captured, the platform quickly lowers into a horizontal position. From here, magnetic pulleys drag the ship forward as the trap rises to receive the next incoming Angel.

Elevators can carry the Angel ship down into the maintenance hangar where each jet has its own individual team of 'whitejackets' – technicians and robots who carry out regular 24-hour checks. Replacement Angel interceptors are also stored and maintained in this hanger, so that Cloudbase always has at least three Angels ready to launch. Beyond the maintenance hanger is the insulated fuel dump, where the highly combustible JP12 is stored. Regular supplies are ferried in from Bensheba by a conventional WAAF tanker, and fed in through a pump nozzle in the hangar wall.

Beyond the fuel dump is the duty hangur, which acts as a base for the Spectrum Passenger Jet. Based on an original design by Universal Aerospace, the SPJ, with a range of twelve thousand miles, is the main method of transport to and from Cloudbase. When Captains Scarlet and Blue must leave on an urgent mission, they taxi the SPJ out of the duty hangar and through an airlock on to the main flight deck. Up above, Angels Two and Three may still be taking off from their own flight deck. Once the Angels have cleared Spectrum air-space, the pilot triggers the twin reheat

engines of the Spectrum Passenger Jet. As the jet moves forward, the nose-wheel prop is caught by the shuttle of a steam catapult which compresses the strut into a 'kneeling' position. As the jet engines fire, the catapult hurls the plane forward and the energy in the compressed nose strut is released, guiding the nose of the SPJ up into the correct take-off position.

As the SPJ flies up and away from Cloudbase, the pilot signs off in Spectrum Code: Spectrum Is Red, if something has gone wrong, or more usually, when everything is proceeding according to plan, Spectrum is Green. SIG!

Mysteronised Angel jets dive over French fields.

THE UNITED COLOURS OF ANDERSON

With attention shifted away from spacecraft and onto characters, *Captain Scarlet and the Mysterons* had the largest regular cast of any Supermarionation series. The characters were not given a complex history, even though the series was the first to be tied in with the 'Anderson world' devised by *TV21*. As Alan Fennell explains, it was left to Angus Allan, Tod Sullivan and other staff working on the annuals to devise a past for the Spectrum agents. 'The film people were more concerned with the visual side, so they didn't have time to produce character profiles. Instead we'd get together round a table and decide where each character should come from.'

Captain Scarlet

Captain Scarlet was born with the name Paul Metcalfe in Winchester in 2036. Metcalfe took degrees in Technology, History and Pure Mathematics at Winchester University before transferring to West Point Military Academy. He joined the World Army Air Force, where he quickly rose to the rank of Colonel. Metcalfe was headhunted by the committee assembling Spectrum in 2066, and assigned the codename of Captain Scarlet. The Captain Scarlet who stars in the TV series is a duplicate of the original, possessing his mind and memory but also indestructible. Scarlet is essentially an easy-going character, always a gentleman when informing the enemy that their plans have failed.

Captain Scarlet relaxes off-set.

Captain Blue

Scarlet's best friend in Spectrum is Captain Blue, whose real name is Adam Svenson. Born August 26th 2035 in Boston, Massachusetts, he is the eldest son of a wealthy financier. After winning a scholarship to Harvard University he disappointed his father by joining the World Aeronautic Society instead of the family firm. After progressing from Test Pilot to Security Officer, he volunteered to join Spectrum. Probably the most quick-witted of Spectrum's agents he is also the most cautious.

Bostonian Adam Svenson, Captain Blue to his workmates, is not only Captain Scarlet's partner, but also his best friend. He also has something of a soft spot for Symphony Angel.

Colonel White

Colonel White is the commander of Spectrum. A former admiral in the World Navy, his real name is Charles Gray. Born in London on July 14th 2017, Colonel White has an almost religious devotion to rules and procedure. Where the other puppets have individual 'smiling' heads, Colonel White has a 'slightly curling lip' head.

Lieutenant Green

Seymour Griffiths, better known as Lieutenant Green, the Cloudbase controller, was born in Trinidad on January 18th 2041. With degrees in Music, Telecommunications and Electrical Engineering, Griffiths joined the World Aquanaut Security Patrol as a hydrophones operator, before being promoted to Marineville's Control Centre. As the man who designed Cloudbase's communication systems, Lieutenant Green is normally too valuable to be assigned field duty. So when a case such as 'Lunarville 7' demands his acknowledged electronics expertise, Lieutenant Green is eager to volunteer.

Colonel White delivers another stirring monologue to Spectrum agents throughout the world from his computerised control desk.

Lieutenant Green (Seymour Griffiths) takes advantage of Colonel White's absence from the Control Room!

Rhapsody Angel

Although there are no female Captains in Spectrum, Cloudbase is protected by its team of women pilots – the Angels. Rather than colours, the Angels are codenamed by 'classical' or 'artistic' codenames. Rhapsody Angel is Dianne Simms. Born in Chelsea on April 20th 2043, she studied Law and Sociology at London University. After working for a solicitor in Manchester she joined Airways Light Freight Agency in Norfolk as a pilot. According to the Angels strip in *Lady Penelope* comic, ALFA went bust and Dianne's last job was to deliver a package to a deserted airfield in Italy. There she meets girl pilots from all over the globe. A voice on a loudspeaker (later revealed to be Lieutenant Green) offers the pilots the chance to train as part of the Angels Air Display Team in their unmarked interceptors. They all accept because, as Dianne says, 'Even in the 21st Century, the best jobs still go to male pilots'.

Symphony Angel

Symphony Angel is Karen Wainwright. Born on January 6th 2042 in Cedar Rapids, Iowa, she joined the Universal Secret Service after graduating early from Yale University. After seven years' service, she resigned to join a small air charter company, from where Spectrum recruited her. As the most impulsive of the Angels, she is taken hostage during an attempt to capture Captain Black in 'Manhunt'. A romantic involvement with Captain Blue is hinted at once or twice during the series.

Destiny Angel

Destiny Angel – Juliette Pointon – was born in Paris on August 23rd 2040. Educated in Rome she later joined the World Army Air Force Intelligence Corps. After three years she resigned to set up her own firm of air freight contractors. Destiny is the most ruthless of the Angels, but the fact that she is called to make a formal identification of Captain Scarlet's body in the first episode suggests that they share a close relationship.

Harmony Angel

Harmony Angel (real name Chan Kwan) was born in Tokyo on June 19th 2042 to Chinese parents. After putting her degrees in Physics and Aerodynamics to practical use by establishing a world record for endurance flying, she took over her father's Air Taxi business.

Melody Angel

Melody Angel is Magnolia Jones. Born on January 10th 2043 in Atlanta, Georgia, she is one of the first black Supermarionation characters. An ex-World Army Air Force pilot, it is her insistence that she saw Goddard's plane hit by lightning that alerts Colonel White to the possibility of Mysteron activity.

Rhapsody Angel (Dianne Simms) relaxes with her fellow Angels in the Amber room. Hailing from 'swinging London' Rhapsody is, of course, sporting the latest Carnaby Street fashions.

Symphony Angel – American Karen Wainwright – is a cool and versatile pilot. Her impetuous nature, however, lands her in trouble on more than one occasion.

Melody Angel: Hailing from America's deep south, Magnolia Jones is a confident and meticulous pilot.

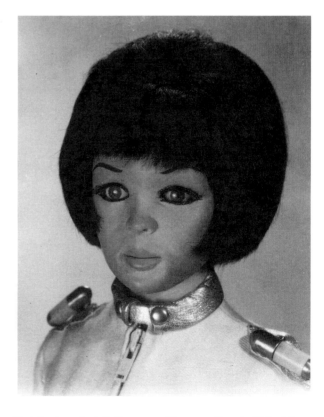

Parisian beauty Juliette Pointon (better known as Destiny Angel) displays a lust for adventure and often acts as Angel leader.

Harmony Angel – Oriental beauty Chan Kwan – is a Judo black belt, as well as being one of Spectrum's most accomplished pilots.

Captain Ochre

Captain Ochre was born Richard Fraser in Detroit on February 23rd 2035. The only Spectrum agent not to attend university, Fraser was turned down by the World Army Air Force because of his lack of formal qualifications. Joining the World Police Corps, Fraser learned to fly in his own time and also carved out a career as a crimebuster. Captain Ochre is more often in charge of personal protection, guarding Conrad Olafsson in 'Codename: Europa' and driving the VIP transporter in 'Dangerous Rendezvous'.

Captain Grey

Captain Grey is the oldest of the Spectrum agents. Born Bradley Holden in Chicago on March 4th 2033, he trained in the World Navy before joining the fledgling World Aquanaut Security Patrol as a Security Commander. Captain Grey is usually seen providing back-up in a variety of Spectrum vehicles, but in 'Winged Assassin' Grey takes centre stage when he saves the Director General of the United Asian Republic from a stealthy Mysteron sniper.

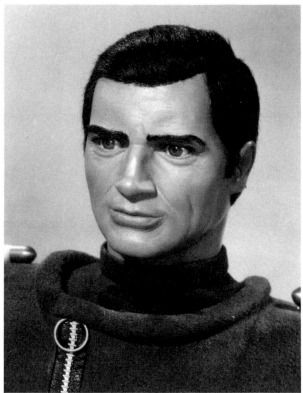

As Captain Ochre, former police chief Richard Fraser specialises in personal security.

Sean Connery lookalike Bradley Holden is better known to his Spectrum colleagues as Captain Grey.

Captain Magenta

Captain Magenta was born in Dublin in 2034 as Patrick Donaghue. His parents emigrated to a tough district of New York when he was only three but despite great poverty he eventually won a scholarship to Yale University. As a student he was briefly jailed for his part in a riot against the totalitarian state of Bereznik, but managed to graduate with degrees in Physics, Electrical Engineering and Information Technology. His first job as a computer programmer offered few challenges and Donaghue turned to crime. However, the Committee which created Spectrum recognised his essential strength of character and offered him the chance to redeem himself. So far, he seems to have justified their gamble. In 'Operation Time' it is Magenta who deciphers the cryptic Mysteron riddle, while in 'Lunarville 7' and 'Crater 101' he replaces the electronics genius, Lieutenant Green, as communications controller.

Doctor Fawn

Whilst on Cloudbase, Edward Wilkie is better known as Doctor Fawn – Spectrum's chief medical officer. Born in Yalumba, Australia on July 10th 2031, he is the son of a famous specialist. After studying medicine at Brisbane University he joined the World Medical Organisation, where he developed the Autonurses seen in *Stingray* episodes.

Captain Black

Officially listed as absent without leave from Spectrum, Captain Black's official file gives his identity as that of Manchester-born orphan Conrad Turner. The biography states that he was raised by a distant relative and received little affection as a child. Despite excelling at college and university, Turner never learned how to display emotion. In 2047 Turner was seriously disfigured by a bomb explosion, while trying to save a British WAAF base from a booby-trap. After his face was reconstructed by plastic surgeons, Turner transferred to the World Space Patrol, where he rose to command Fireball XL3. Yet Spectrum appears to be concealing a deeper mystery about Captain Black; despite being raised in Lancashire, Black's voice in the pilot episode is clearly that of an American.

A graduate of Yale University, Patrick Donaghue joined the Spectrum ranks as Captain Magenta.

Man or Mysteron? As one of Spectrum's top agents, Captain Black (Conrad Turner) was chosen to lead the doomed Zero X mission to Mars.

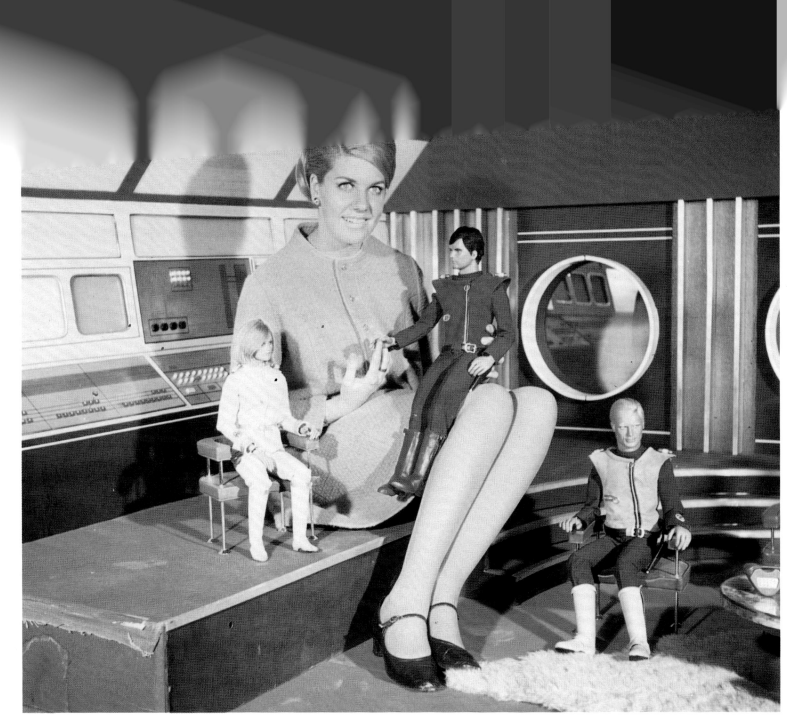

As the puppets were less caricatured in this series, the tendency was also towards more realistic voice portrayals. To play Captain Scarlet, Gerry Anderson chose Francis Matthews, who had recently played the hero of Hammer Films' *Dracula Prince of Darkness* (1966). Born in York, Francis Matthews had a well-established stage and TV career before Captain Scarlet. He starred as Ranjit Kasel opposite Ava Gardner in MGM's *Bhowani Junction* (1956) and played Peter Cushing's apprentice, Hans Kleve, in *The Revenge of Frankenstein* (1957).

Francis Matthews was not auditioned for the role of Scarlet. 'Gerry Anderson had heard me at some time doing an impersonation of Cary Grant and decided that was the voice he wanted for his new hero.' He recalls that although Gerry Anderson didn't move heaven and earth to get him he certainly came close to it. 'At the time of the first two recording sessions I had to be flown up and down to Manchester where I was appearing in Coward's *Private Lives*.' Presumably, this provoked Captain Scarlet's quip that, 'I wouldn't exactly call Manchester the Place of the Angels.'

Following Captain Scarlet, Francis Matthews played the BBC detective Paul Temple for four seasons. Although subsequently offered more action-adventure roles he turned them down, finally accepting 'with relief' a multiple role in Alan Plater's *Trinity Tales*, an update of the

When Cloudbase receives a glamorous guest, Scarlet, Blue and Symphony Angel find themselves entertaining one of their biggest fans!

Canterbury Tales for BBC 2. Since then, Francis Matthews has appeared in over 40 films, countless plays and the most recent series of Scottish Television's *Taggart*.

Captain Blue's voice was provided by New York-born Ed Bishop, whose first film role was opposite Steve McQueen in *The War Lover*. This was followed by two astronaut roles in *2001: A Space Odyssey* and *Mouse on the Moon*. Following *Captain Scarlet*, Ed Bishop went on to star as Commander Straker in Anderson's first live action series *UFO* (1970). Still much in demand as an actor, Ed Bishop has appeared in *The Mad Death* (BBC Scotland), *The Professionals* (LWT) and *Canned Carrott* (BBC), as well as playing Raymond Chandler's *Philip Marlowe* for BBC radio.

Donald Grey was the voice of Colonel White – and also the voice of Captain Black and the Mysterons. Born Eldred Tilbury in 1914, Donald Grey starred in the 1939 version of *The Four Feathers*, as one of the blood-and-thunder buddies who present John Clements with the white feathers of the title. In 1957, he began starring as one-armed detective *Mark Saber* in the long-running Danziger production. Having lost an arm during the war, his voice was arguably Grey's greatest asset: he was able to suggest the essential good nature behind Colonel White's bureaucratic and crusty exterior.

Cy Grant, who voiced Lieutenant Green, had his first starring role in John Elliott's *Man From the Sun*, a BBC play about West Indian immigrants in England. He later achieved fame as a calypso singer in the BBC's magazine programme *Tonight*. Following Captain Scarlet, he appeared as a head of state in *The Persuaders!*, Dayna's father in *Blake's Seven* and a Pellucidan leader in *At The Earth's Core*.

Elizabeth Morgan voiced both Destiny and Rhapsody Angels. At the time she was best known for presenting a schools programme called *Finding Out*. She recalls that acting for puppet voice-overs was more challenging than ordinary radio work because the puppets themselves were restricted in their display of emotions. 'During one session, Rhapsody Angel was worrying about some life or death situation that was threatening Captain Scarlet. I was close to tears and I was told, "Puppets can't cry Liz . . . do it

Captain Brown – one of Spectrum's leading agents until the Mysterons turned him into a living bomb.

another way!".' Since Scarlet she has written over 24 plays for BBC Radio 4 and has taken her one-woman shows to America and the National Theatre. She appeared in *The Old Devils* for BBC Wales and was Joanna the District Nurse in both series of HTV's *We Are Seven*.

Captain Ochre's voice was furnished by Jeremy Wilkin who succeeded David Holliday as Virgil Tracy in the last six episodes of *Thunderbirds* and the two feature films. In 1965 Jeremy Wilkin had starred as Drewe Herriot in the ABC fantasy thriller, *Undermind*. He stayed with Century 21 Productions for *Joe 90* and *The Secret Service* (in which he played The Bishop), whilst in 1970 he donned a green string vest to become a

Jason Smith, Mysteronised firefighter, prepares to destroy Spectrum's oil refinery. He was one of the characters voiced by David Healy.

Skydiver navigator in *UFO*. Apart from guest starring in *Doctor Who* and *The New Avengers*, Wilkin returned to voice-over work for Halas and Batchelor's RAI cartoon series, *The Count of Monte Cristo*. Wilkin also provided the voice of the human Captain Black, during the opening scenes of 'The Mysterons'.

Paul Maxwell provided the voice of Captain Grey, the World President and several 'guest-stars' in the series. A naturalised American, Paul Maxwell was actually born in Canada and first came to Britain with the Commonwealth forces during World War Two. Maxwell's rich expansive tones will probably always be associated with Colonel Steve Zodiac of *Fireball XL5* but he also provided the voice of Paul Travers, the Zero X commander in *Thunderbirds Are Go!* By co-incidence, Paul Maxwell was also appearing in *Coronation Street* during the summer of 1967. As Steve Tanner he was brought into the show specifically to marry Elsie Tanner (Pat Phoenix). Their TV wedding, drawing a massive audience, took place on September 4th 1967, only a month before Scarlet's TV premiere. Subsequently, Paul Maxwell played Lt. Lewis, a Skydiver crewman, in the *UFO* episode 'Sub-Smash'. He continued to work in film and TV, appearing as the Man with the White Hat in the opening sequence of *Indiana Jones And The Last Crusade*.

Playing Captain Magenta was Gary Files. Australian born, but a naturalised Canadian, Files had appeared in *The Spies* and *Softly Softly* for the BBC before landing the role of Captain Magenta. He also substituted for Ray Barrett in the role of John Tracy in the film *Thunderbird Six*. Subsequently, he played Matthew, the six-inch spy in *The Secret Service*, character voices in *Joe 90* and Phil Wade in the first episode of *UFO*. Since returning to Australia, Gary Files has played a variety of stage roles from the manic DJ Leonard Brasil in *City Sugar* to the Joe McCarthy figure in *Insignificance*. He appeared alongside Charles Tingwell in *The Money Movers* (1978), but to *Neighbours* fans Gary Files will be best known for his rare appearances as Tom Ramsey.

The voice of Doctor Fawn and the ill-fated Captain Brown was Charles Tingwell, star of ATV's *Emergency Ward Ten* from 1957 to 1968. Tingwell appeared as Inspector Craddock in the Miss Marple movies (including *Murder Ahoy* in 1964, with Francis Matthews) and also played the brother of Francis Matthews in *Dracula Prince of Darkness* (1966). Despite an extremely busy schedule, Tingwell had found the time to record character voices for the last six episodes of *Thunderbirds* and the movie, *Thunderbirds Are Go!* Tingwell later starred in *Catweazle* and the 'Mindbender' episode of *UFO*. In the 1970s he returned to Australia, where as Charles 'Bud' Tingwell he appeared in many movie roles including

Rod Dexter: Hollywood stars were too expensive for *Captain Scarlet*, even as puppets, but this Robert Mitchum lookalike played support in several episodes such as *The Trap* and *Fire at Rig 15*.

gang leader Jack Henderson in Bruce Beresford's *The Money Movers* (1978).

Although each regular character had his own voice artiste, (with Janna Hill playing Symphony Angel, Sylvia Anderson playing Melody and Lian-Shin performing some of Harmony's lines) the 'supporting players' were voiced either by the 'second leads', such as Tingwell and Maxwell, or specially drafted actors. Shane Rimmer can be heard providing uncredited voices in 'Special Assignment' and 'Flight to Atlantica' while Martin King and David Healy played the 'guest-stars'. Healy in particular leapt on the opportunity to step outside the casting restrictions which usually applied to American actors in ITC series. His roles range from the Australian fire-fighter Jason Smith in 'Fire At Rig 15' to the bull-headed President Roberts in 'The Launching'. Following Captain Scarlet, Healy played the dead gangster Bugsy Spanio in *Randall and Hopkirk (Deceased)*, Nicely Nicely in the National Theatre's *Guys and Dolls*, the voice of Shane Weston in *Joe 90*, and even an English mercenary in an episode of *Charlie's Angels*.

'WE WILL BE AVENGED . . .'

Captain Scarlet's fight against the Mysterons was to last for thirty-two episodes, each with an on-screen running time of approximately twenty-five minutes. The structure of the episodes is notable for the fact that, with the exception of the pilot story, they each boast two opening title sequences.

The opening titles are seen over an eerie and largely symbolic sequence, in which Captain Scarlet is introduced and his indestructible nature established. Early versions of this sequence were mainly silent, whilst the majority featured an introductory voice-over by Ed Bishop.

The secondary title sequence (over which the voice of the Mysterons issued its weekly threat) followed the episode's 'teaser' and introduced the viewer to Captain Blue, Colonel White and the five Angels. The omnipotent nature of the Mysterons is stressed, as the familiar twin circles drift over the oblivious Spectrum personnel. The sequence ends with another largely symbolic shot, this time of a uniformed Captain Black standing in a mist-shrouded graveyard.

Each episode ended with the Captain Scarlet theme, composed by Barry Gray. Early episodes of the series featured a predominantly instrumental version: the words 'Captain Scarlet' repeated at regular intervals in an unearthly, electronic voice, which was produced by Barry Gray using a ring-modulator (a device which imposes complex patterns on any sound which passes through it). Most of the episodes, however, closed with the well-remembered vocal arrangement of the theme, performed by The Spectrum, the group

formed by Gerry Anderson purely as a marketing exercise. Both versions of the theme were accompanied by excellent colour paintings by *TV21* artist Ron Embleton, showing a grim-faced Captain Scarlet in a number of spectacular and seemingly fatal situations.

The following chapter covers all thirty-two episodes of the series, presented in their original order of transmission. The episode title is followed by the often cryptic Mysteron threat-of-the-week.

Lurking doom: Scarlet suspects a Mysteron ambush.

Death hides in the shadows as Captain Black sets his sights on another unfortunate victim.

 **The Mysterons**

'Our first act of retaliation will be to assassinate your World President.'

It is the year 2068 and, following what they mistakenly believe to be an attack on their Martian city, the Mysterons declare war on mankind. As Earth's first line of defence, the Spectrum organisation swings into action, but not before Captains Scarlet and Brown are killed and their Mysteron duplicates dispatched on a mission of death. Surviving an attempt on his life by Captain Brown exploding beside him the World President is placed under the protection of Captain Scarlet – who proceeds to kidnap him and take him to the top of the 800-foot high London Car-Vu. Pursued and eventually shot by Captain Blue, Scarlet falls to his death but, upon recovery of the body, Spectrum make a startling discovery! Scarlet is mysteriously able to regenerate himself and live to continue Spectrum's fight against the Mysterons – unwittingly the Mysterons have created Spectrum's most important weapon.

One of the many points of interest in this episode is the unusual shot of Harmony Angel preparing to board her aircraft. Following Lieutenant Green's order for immediate launch, Harmony is seen moving towards her chair, located behind the double glass doors in the amber room. The stringless puppet is then viewed from behind and shown to sit down in the chair, which then slides back into the elevator-shaft. An effective shot which was never re-used. Also worth mentioning is the 'grimacing' Captain Scarlet who is seen to fall from the London Car-Vu, having been shot by Captain Blue during the episode's climactic battle. By using a highly detailed landscape, an amazing sense of perspective is achieved for the shot in which Scarlet is seen to plummet towards the ground!

Teleplay by Gerry & Sylvia Anderson
Directed by Desmond Saunders

2 Winged Assassin

'We will assassinate the Director General of the United Asian Republic.'

As the elected leader of two hundred million people, the life of the Mysterons' latest target has to be safeguarded at all costs. Following an unsuccessful attempt by an agile sniper, Spectrum make arrangements to transfer the Director General of the United Asian Republic from his London hotel to his private jet at London International Airport. On Cloudbase, Captain Scarlet makes a full recovery after his fall from the London Car-Vu and, together with Captain Blue, is sent back to the city to take part in the operation. Despite elaborate precautions, the Mysterons are one step ahead and, as Scarlet, Blue and the Control Tower staff look on, a Mysteronised Stratojet breaks away from its terminal and heads on a collision course with the Director General's plane. Scarlet must prove he is invincible and save the Director General.

Continuity buffs will no doubt make much of this episode's July 10th dateline, as it is also the date given during the much later 'Treble Cross'.

Teleplay by Tony Barwick
Directed by David Lane

3 Big Ben Strikes Again

'Our next act of retaliation will be to destroy the city of London.'

It is almost midnight and a high destruction-ratio atomic device is being transported through London; its destination, an underground construction site ten miles outside of the city. At the wheel of the huge transporter, the driver, Macey, can only watch helplessly as his vehicle seems to take on a life of its own, careering madly through the streets, before coming to a sudden stop in an underground car park. Finding himself sealed in, Macey switches on his radio and is baffled to hear Big Ben strike thirteen times! Suddenly aware that he is no longer alone, Macey is struck from behind and knocked unconscious, but not before he has seen the atomic device become fully armed – turning it into a bomb of devastating power. Naturally, Captain Scarlet is the only hope to deal with the deadly situation.

Teleplay by Tony Barwick
Directed by Brian Burgess

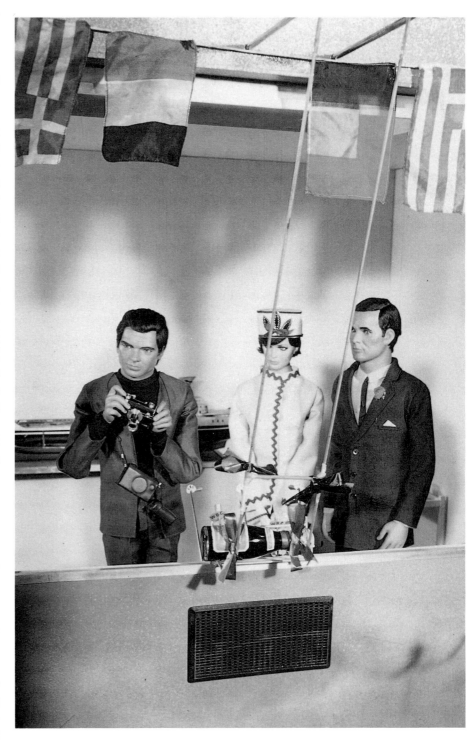

Mysteron Mervin Brand (with the camera) made an earlier appearance as Macey in the episode *Big Ben Strikes Again*.

A Mysteron scheme is foiled when, having broken into the Culver Atomic Centre, Captain Black is discovered and forced to beat a hasty retreat. On Cloudbase, Colonel White reveals that, during his escape, Captain Black exposed himself to a short-life atomic isotope, meaning that, for the next 48 hours the Mysteron agent will be a source of radioactivity. Using special detector trucks, equipped with directional, long-range Geiger Counters, Spectrum closes the net around the fleeing Black, but not before he steals an SPV and takes Symphony Angel as a hostage!

It is unclear exactly what Captain Black hoped to achieve by breaking into the Culver Atomic Centre as, unlike every other episode in the series, 'Manhunt' didn't feature a specific Mysteron threat or announcement; instead, the secondary title sequence was accompanied only by a re-iterated promise that the Mysteron retaliation would be '. . . slow, but none the less effective.'

Also worth noting are the frequent requests by Lieutenant Green that he be allowed to join in the manhunt. Colonel White refuses, but eventually relents, as the following episode shows.

Teleplay by Tony Barwick
Directed by Alan Perry

5 Avalanche

'We will destroy key-links in your Frost Line Outer Space Defence System.'

When the Mysterons threaten the Alaskan chain of missile complexes and observation posts, the Frost Line commander, General Ward, promises massive retaliation if any of his installations are attacked. Concerned about the consequences should Ward launch a strike against Mars, Colonel White sends Captain Scarlet and Lieutenant Green to investigate, when contact with one of the missile bases is suddenly lost. Arriving at the base, the Spectrum men discover that a Mysteron agent has sabotaged the air-conditioning system. As Lieutenant Green repairs the damage, Captain Scarlet must prevent the saboteur from reaching the Command Base.

A notable episode, in that while Captain Blue remains on Cloudbase at the communications console, Lieutenant Green accompanies Scarlet on his mission. No on-screen reason for this is given, although it is safe to assume that Colonel White sent him along in response to his requests during the previous story.

Teleplay by Shane Rimmer
Directed by Brian Burgess

Rolling thunder: the virtually indestructible Spectrum Pursuit Vehicle.

6 White As Snow

'Our next act of retaliation will be to kill the Commander in Chief of Spectrum, Colonel White.'

Following an unsuccessful attempt to destroy Cloudbase – the Mysterons having set a communications satellite on a collision course – Colonel White announces that, in order to safeguard the lives of everyone else on the base, he is to leave for a secret destination. The Mysterons, as ever, prove difficult to thwart and, no sooner has Colonel White made contact with a World Navy submarine than one of the crew dies in an accident – his Mysteron duplicate being assigned to look after the Colonel during the voyage!

An amusing episode in which Captain Blue is given the opportunity of commanding Cloudbase in Colonel White's absence. No doubt aware that his newly-acquired status will be short-lived, the Captain clearly enjoys himself by organising unpopular lectures and repeatedly sending the Angels to carry out target practice.

Teleplay by Peter Curran & David Williams
Directed by Robert Lynn

Colonel Whites takes to the sea in an attempt to elude the Mysterons.

The Trap

'At the appointed hour, as the clock is chiming, the wings of the world will be clipped.'

Spectrum is assigned to provide the security for an international air conference, at which all the high ranking officers of the World Airforce are to discuss methods for dealing with the Mysteron menace. En route to Cloudbase, the plane carrying Air Commodore Goddard crashes, having been struck by lightning, and it is a Mysteron duplicate which eventually completes the journey. Colonel White is surprised when Goddard announces that he has changed the location of the conference to the isolated Glengarry Castle in Scotland, but accepts the decision and sends Captain Scarlet to the castle with Goddard to check security. Making a search of the Banqueting Hall, Scarlet discovers a heavy-duty machine gun concealed behind a huge painting; manned by Holte (Goddard's pilot) the weapon is trained on the table at which the delegates are due to meet. Bound and gagged, Scarlet is helpless as, using his voice, the Mysteronised Air Commodore contacts Cloudbase and informs Colonel White that it is safe for the conference to begin.

Making its one and only appearance in this story is the Magnacopter. Looking more like a submarine than an aircraft, the incredible machine clearly belongs to the World Airforce, although Symphony Angel is given the sought-after job of piloting it to and from the conference.

Worth noting is a mix of live action and puppetry in order to create the illusion of great depth for the scene in which Captain Scarlet and Symphony are discovered in the castle dungeon.

Teleplay by Alan Pattillo
Directed by Alan Perry

Imprisoned within the dungeon of Glengarry Castle, Scarlet and Symphony must warn the conference delegates that they have walked into a trap.

 Operation Time

'Our next act of retaliation will be to kill time.'

In an exclusive London clinic, General Tiempo, Commander of the Western Region World Defence, is due to undergo a brain operation, under the supervision of Professor Magnus, a pioneering surgeon who has developed a revolutionary piece of apparatus known as the Cerebral Pulsator. Night falls and tragedy strikes, as, driving home, Professor Magnus dies when his car is forced off the road by Captain Black. Now merely a soulless puppet, the Mysteronised Magnus returns to the clinic with one purpose only – to kill General Tiempo.

A 'key' episode of the series, in which we discover the Mysterons' Achilles' heel – they are impervious to X-rays and can easily be killed by a high voltage electric current. The episode is also notable for those with a particular interest in the layout of Cloudbase, as it reveals that both the Sick Bay and Generator Room are on deck C.

Teleplay by Richard Conway
& Stephen J. Mattick
Directed by Ken Turner

9 Spectrum Strikes Back

'You will never solve the mystery of the Mysterons.'

Colonel White, Captain Scarlet and Captain Blue travel to the secret headquarters of the Spectrum Intelligence Agency, where Dr Giardello demonstrates two new advances in the fight against the Mysterons: the portable Mysteron Detector and the Anti-Mysteron Electron Gun. As the assembled delegates watch the demonstration, Captain Black arrives and kills Captain Indigo and it's not long before the new devices are put to the test.

Intended as a sequel to 'Operation Time', Spectrum's newly developed Anti-Mysteron devices make their first (and in the case of the Electron Gun, only) appearance. 'This is the only gun that kills a Mysteron,' announces Scarlet, as he zaps Captain Indigo. Strange, then, that it is never seen again – conventional bullets proving to be adequate for the remainder of the series.

Teleplay by Tony Barwick
Directed by Ken Turner

10 Special Assignment

'We intend to obliterate the sub-continent of North America.'

Spectrum personnel are expressly forbidden to gamble, so when Captain Scarlet loses $5,000 at the Dice Club casino, Colonel White has no choice but to ask for his resignation. Destitute and with nowhere to go, Scarlet returns to the scene of his downfall and, at the seedy Gregory hotel, meets a couple of racketeers who promise to cancel his debts in return for an SPV. Accompanying the villains to a remote ranch house, Scarlet discovers that they are Mysterons and is informed, by Captain Black, that they intend to use the stolen SPV to destroy Nuclear City. But the jigsaw is not yet complete . . .

An unusual episode which contains more than one red herring. For example, how did Spectrum know in advance that the two racketeers running the casino were Mysterons? The answer is that a Spectrum Intelligence agent is working undercover at the drab Vincent Bar, so obviously he overheard the two Mysterons plotting!

Teleplay by Tony Barwick
Directed by Robert Lynn

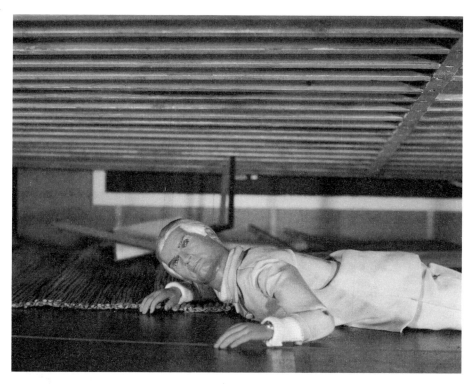

A pressing engagement for Colonel White when a Mysteron agent brings the house down.

Unable to watch, Captain Blue turns away as Scarlet loses everything on the roulette wheel.

11 The Heart of New York

'We've seen the greed and corruption of the world in which you live and will take our revenge upon it.'

When three crooks break into the Spectrum Security Vault, they come away with nothing but microfilm and classified documents. Their haul seems useless, until their leader discovers that it contains detailed information about the Mysterons and their powers of reconstruction. The Mysterons, meanwhile, announce that they are to attack New York – the city is evacuated and Spectrum personnel sent in to patrol the deserted streets. Using their newly-acquired information, the crooks convince Spectrum that the Mysterons' target is the Second National Bank. Colonel White is unwilling to risk Spectrum lives to protect a bank and so orders his agents to withdraw. With nothing to stand in their way, the crooks enter the unguarded bank and prepare to make off with a fortune in gold . . .

The Spectrum personal radio receiver makes its one and only appearance in this episode. Manning a road block on the outskirts of New York, Captain Magenta dons a pair of sporty sunglasses, the arms of which contain tiny speakers which allow him to hear the voice of Captain Ochre, who is concealed nearby.

Teleplay by Tony Barwick
Directed by Alan Perry

12 Lunarville 7

'We have no quarrel with the moon and we accept their offer of friendship.'

Together with Lieutenant Green, Captains Scarlet and Blue are sent to the moon to investigate claims by the Lunar Controller that he has established contact with the Mysterons and succeeded in coming to a peaceful agreement. As night falls, the three Spectrum men steal a moon mobile and head for an area on the dark side of the moon, known as the Humboldt Sea, as it is from here

that strange signals have been detected. As the moon mobile reaches the edge of a huge crater, the earthmen are unable to believe their eyes. Within the crater, moving with an ominous sense of purpose, bizarre machines are seen scuttling about, engrossed in their task – the construction of a new Mysteron city!

A good episode and the first of three ('Crater 101' and 'Dangerous Rendezvous' being the others), 'Lunarville 7' features the voice of Gerry Anderson himself as the Lunarville computer, SID!

Teleplay by Tony Barwick
Directed by Robert Lynn

When they break into the Second National Bank, this trio of crooks discover that impersonating Mysterons carries a high price.

A bug-like moon mobile – ideal for lunar tours and unofficial excursions to the Humboldt Sea.

Fashion designer André Verdain entertains two of his favourite models.

13 Point 783

'We shall destroy the Supreme Commander of Earth Forces within the next twenty-four hours.'

In order to counter the latest Mysteron threat, Captains Scarlet and Blue are assigned to protect the endangered Commander. Travelling with Captain Blue to Point 783, a remote Command Post in the Sahara Desert, the Supreme Commander watches as the new Unitron tank is put through its paces. Unmanned and completely impervious to attack, the Unitron is the ultimate weapon of war. What chance do the observers have, therefore, when the tank veers off course and opens fire on the unprotected bunker . . .

A point of note: doesn't the Command Post interior look like *UFO*'s SHADO control room? Clearly Supervising Art Director Bob Bell was pleased with his own work and decided that a full-sized version of the design was just the place to base Ed Straker and his underground defence force.

Teleplay by Peter Curran & David Williams
Directed by Robert Lynn

14 Model Spy

'We are about to attack the House of Verdain.'

Why should the Mysterons wish to kill top fashion designer André Verdain? Perhaps it's because he is a spy for the European Area Intelligence Agency and has been trailing Captain Black for months. Going undercover, Captains Scarlet and Blue, together with Destiny and Symphony Angels, travel to sunny Monte Carlo, where Verdain is putting on a fashion show. Unbeknown to everyone, two of Verdain's top models are now in the hands of the Mysterons and waste no time in acting upon the instructions of their new masters . . .

A *Man from UNCLE*-type episode in which Scarlet and Blue don their civvies for an unusual assignment on the French Riviera. A nice break from the routine and some convincing antics from a couple of stringless puppets towards the end.

Teleplay by Bill Hedley
Directed by Ken Turner

Ditched! Scarlet, Blue and Destiny Angel come under fire from Mysteronised Angel aircraft.

. . . and this is how it was done! Dry-ice and powerful lights are used to create an explosive effect.

Designed to overcome all forms of defence, a Mysteron-controlled Variable Geometry Rocket homes in on its own base.

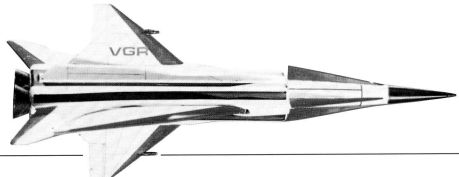

 15 Seek and Destroy

'We intend to kill one of the Spectrum Angels.'

Unaware that three unfinished Angel Aircraft have been destroyed in a fire, Colonel White sends Captains Scarlet and Blue to Paris, to pick up a holidaying Destiny Angel and return her to the safety of Cloudbase. En route to the airport, Scarlet and his colleagues are attacked by the Mysteronised aircraft and, from the safety of a roadside ditch, they watch as the real Spectrum Angels are engaged in a deadly battle with three perfectly matched opponents.

Featuring plenty of spectacular aerial sequences, this episode turns out to be an excellent showcase for the Angel Aircraft, as well as providing the small 'Flying Unit' of Century 21 with an opportunity to express themselves in full.

Teleplay by Peter Curran & David Williams
Directed by Alan Perry

 16 Renegade Rocket

'We are going to launch one of your own incendiary rockets and you will have no way of knowing its target.'

On his way to Base Concorde, an island-based rocket installation, Space Major Reeves is killed by Captain Black – a Mysteron duplicate immediately taking his place. Once in the Rocket Control Room, he launches a Variable Geometry Rocket: a missile designed to overcome all forms of defence in order to reach its target. Arriving at the base, Captains Scarlet and Blue are on hand as the rocket suddenly reappears on the radar and it is discovered that Base Concorde is its target.

Having gained access to the Control Room at Base Concorde, Major Reeves is seen to shoot the missile technician with Captain Scarlet's colour-coded pistol. Strange – these personalised guns are never supposed to leave the side of their owner!

Teleplay by Ralph Hart
Directed by Brian Burgess

On Lunarville 6 Linda Nolan points the way as the Spectrum trio plan to infiltrate the Mysteron's moon city.

 17 **Crater 101**

'Although you have discovered our complex on the moon, it will never reveal its secrets.'

Returning to the moon, Captain Scarlet, Captain Blue and Lieutenant Green set off from Lunarville 6 to penetrate the newly discovered Mysteron complex. Once inside, they have to find and remove the power source before the installation can be destroyed by an atomic device. Unbeknown to the three agents, the driver of the Lunar Tank is a Mysteron and the bomb which he is bringing has been set to explode one hour ahead of schedule.

The sequel to 'Lunarville 7', this episode carries a couple of interesting technical points. First, the interior of the moon mobile seen in this episode differs slightly from the one used before. Where the Lunarville 7 mobile was controlled by twin joy-sticks, this one features two steering columns. Second, the scene in which the Mysteronised Frazer departs the moonbase in a Lunar Tank is also technically noteworthy, as the domed building glimpsed in the background is, in fact, the camera-housing of the Mini-Sat which would be featured in the following story.

Teleplay by Tony Barwick
Directed by Ken Turner

Inside the Mysteron complex, Lieutenant Green stands transfixed by a hypnotic screen.

Astronomer Doctor Breck takes a close look at Mars. Nothing can prepare him for what he is about to see.

18 Shadow of Fear

'You will never discover the secret of the Mysterons.'

In order to obtain close-up pictures of Mars, astronomers soft-land a mini satellite on the Martian moon Phobos. At an isolated observatory, high in the Himalayan Mountains, Captains Scarlet and Blue keep watch and wait for the revealing pictures to be transmitted back to Earth. When one of the astronomers disappears, Captain Scarlet suspects it to be the work of the Mysterons and sets out to find him before he can sabotage the whole operation.

A pioneer in the use of electronic music and effects, composer Barry Gray produced an eerie score for this episode which adds considerably to the space sequences. Not surprisingly, much of this score is used later in *UFO*.

Teleplay by Tony Barwick
Directed by Robert Lynn

19 Dangerous Rendezvous

'Spectrum Headquarters Cloudbase will be destroyed at midnight.'

By using the diamond pulsator power-source taken from the Mysterons' lunar complex, Colonel White succeeds in communicating with the inhabitants of Mars. In replying to his offer of friendship, the Mysterons insist that a lone, unarmed member of Spectrum meets their representative at a location of their choice. Aware that he could be walking into a trap, Captain Scarlet volunteers for the crucial assignment.

This is an interesting episode as it features a detailed explanation and demonstration of the unique cap-mike communications system. The recipient of this demonstration, the scientist Dr Kurnitz, is also treated to a specially arranged Angel launch, which, bearing in mind that Cloudbase has just been threatened, seems a fairly unwise thing to do!

With the help of Doctor Kurnitz, Colonel White prepares to communicate with the Mysterons.

Teleplay by Tony Barwick
Directed by Brian Burgess

20 Fire at Rig 15

'We intend to immobilise the whole of Spectrum.'

In order to carry out their latest threat, the Mysterons cause a fire at Spectrum's Bensheba Oil Refinery. Arriving at the rig, Captains Scarlet and Blue watch as ace fire-fighter Jason Smith succeeds in blowing the fire out with high explosives. Unbeknown to them, however, it is a Mysteronised Smith who walks away from the now safely gushing oil well, the real fire-fighter having fallen under the influence of Captain Black and perished in the explosion.

A good example of deceptive model work can be seen near the beginning of this episode, when Captains Scarlet and Blue leave Cloudbase in a Spectrum Passenger Jet, escorted by an Angel flight. As the Angels close in around the jet, Captain Blue watches Angel 2 glide into view, apparently several yards from the plane. In fact, what the viewer is seeing is a scale model, no larger than Captain Blue himself, being suspended only inches from the cockpit set.

Teleplay by Bryan Cooper
Directed by Ken Turner

21 Treble Cross

'We will destroy the world capital – Futura City.'

When Captain Black attempts to kill ace test-pilot Major Gravener, he reckons without two pioneering doctors, who pull the comatose man from his watery grave and bring him back to life. Unaware that his human counterpart is alive, the Mysteronised Gravener returns to Slaton airbase and requisitions an XK107 bomber – complete with armed nuclear warhead. When the real Major Gravener turns up, he joins Spectrum in a daring plan to deceive the Mysterons.

Realism was important to Gerry Anderson and his team and, during the making of this series, efforts were made to ensure that the puppets were

as believable as possible. A good example of this is the puppet of Major Gravener which, thanks to a small air-bag hidden beneath his bedclothes, is seen to breathe deeply as he lies within the hospital Recovery Unit.

Teleplay by Tony Barwick
Directed by Alan Perry

 Flight 104

'The conference at Lake Toma will be sabotaged.'

Captains Scarlet and Blue are assigned to escort the leading astrophysicist Dr Conrad to a special conference in Switzerland – the purpose of the conference, to decide the method and purpose of man's return to Mars. On the way to Geneva airport, Scarlet makes a startling discovery: the flightdeck of the plane in which they are travelling is empty. As Scarlet and Blue wrestle with the controls, a hazardous mountain range looms into sight and they realise that there is nothing they can do to prevent a crash.

A point worth noting is that this episode features a small amount of footage from *Thunderbirds* when, towards the end fire tenders are seen rushing to aid the imperilled airliner.

Teleplay by Tony Barwick
Directed by Robert Lynn

Captain Scarlet, following his attempt to land the Mysteron-controlled airliner in *Flight 104*.

Laboratory assistant Judy Chapman gets to grips with a deadly man-made virus.

Kitted out in a thermal pressure suit, Captain Scarlet goes after the Mysteron saboteur who has imperilled the Hot Spot Tower.

 23 Place of Angels

'**We will destroy the place of the Angels.**'

Judy Chapman, laboratory assistant at a bacteriological research centre, falls under Mysteron control and steals a phial of K14 – a newly developed culture, capable of causing death on a massive scale. Throwing off her pursuers, Chapman arrives at the Boulder Dam on the Colorado river and, as a wounded Captain Scarlet parachutes on to the scene, she prepares to contaminate the entire water supply of Los Angeles.

Composer Barry Gray produced some extremely effective music for the series, but time was always tight and, occasionally, it would be necessary to use appropriate pieces of earlier scores. The dramatic music which can be heard as Dr Denton mixes the K14 virus will be familiar to fans of *Stingray* as one of the earlier series' recurring themes.

Teleplay by Leo Eaton
Directed by Leo Eaton

 24 Noose of Ice

'**We will make sure that you never return to our planet, Mars.**'

Deep below the polar ice cap, scientists are drilling for Tritonium alloy – a rare metal essential for the new space fleet bound for Mars. Massive heating elements keep the surrounding water at a constant 60 degrees, thus preventing the ice from closing in and crushing the installation. When a Mysteron saboteur cuts off the power supply, Captain Scarlet must race against the forces of nature in order to avert disaster.

With a limited amount of space in which to build sets, the series' principal vehicles and buildings were modelled in a variety of different sizes and used depending upon the requirements of any particular scene.

Teleplay by Tony Barwick
Directed by Ken Turner

 25 Expo 2068

'Disaster will strike the Atlantic seaboard of North America. We will deal a heavy blow to the prestige of the world.'

When a nuclear reactor disappears during transit, Spectrum suspect it to be the work of the Mysterons. Tracing the stolen device to the site of Expo 2068 – a massive world trade fair – Captain Scarlet must gain entry to a hovering cargo-copter and defuse the potentially explosive situation.

This episode is significant as being the only one in which real black and white television screens are used as monitors, instead of the usual mock-up flat-screens, brought to life by convincing visual trickery.

Teleplay by Shane Rimmer
Directed by Leo Eaton

 26 The Launching

'We will destroy President Roberts within the next twelve hours.'

Assuming that the Mysterons intend to assassinate the head of state, Colonel White dispatches Captains Scarlet and Blue to throw a security cordon around his residence. As Scarlet tries to convince the President that he is in mortal danger, little does he know that a Mysteron agent is already in the area – his sights set on a far bigger target.

Whilst it was usual for model aircraft to be suspended from wires in order to simulate flight, this episode contains a scene which suggests that this wasn't always so. As Rhapsody and Destiny fly past Mysteron Brand's jet, it is apparent that the Angel aircraft are attached as a suitably clever alternative to the rapidly moving backdrop.

Teleplay by Peter Curran & David Williams
Directed by Brian Burgess

Electronics genius and
Mysteron agent Gabriel
Carney cuts his way into a
Spectrum Security Centre.
Can Scarlet and Blue stop
him wiping out the
Triumvirate of Europe?

 **27 Codename Europa**

'The triumvirate of Europe will be destroyed.'

John L. Henderson, Conrad Olafsson and Joseph Maccini; after the World President, the most powerful men on earth – and now marked for death. Concealing the men in separate security establishments, Spectrum are confident of beating the latest Mysteron threat. But they have reckoned without the skills of an electronics genius, Gabriel Carney, now on the side of the Mysterons, who soon turns out to be a formidable opponent.

In order to add that extra touch of authenticity, small figures were often used on the model set, which would have been far too small to accommodate full-sized puppets. A swivelling model of Captain Magenta is put to good use during the scene in which the Mysteronised Professor Carney spectacularly crashes his car through a Spectrum road block.

Teleplay by David Lee
Directed by Alan Perry

 **28 Inferno**

'Our next act of retaliation will be to destroy the complex at Najama.'

When the Mysterons threaten a desalination plant in the Andean foothills, Captains Scarlet and Blue set up camp in an old Aztec temple and mount a round-the-clock vigil. In space, a Mysteronised recovery vehicle plummets towards the earth – its re-entry computer homing in on a transmitting device which Captain Black has concealed in a very unusual place.

Obviously keen to establish the existence of a European space operation in addition to the obvious American space programme, the writers of this episode placed the SKR4 recovery vehicle firmly under the control of an agency known as Euro-Space.

Teleplay by Tony Barwick & Shane Rimmer
Directed by Alan Perry

 **29 Traitor**

'The Spectrum organisation will be torn apart from within.'

When the Mysterons announce that a traitor will create havoc for Spectrum, Colonel White sends Captains Scarlet and Blue to Koala Base, Australia, where a number of mysterious hovercraft accidents have resulted in the deaths of several men. Joining the crew of hovercraft number 4, the Spectrum captains travel deep into the Australian outback, recreating the exact conditions surrounding the previous crash. It is then that disaster strikes.

The superbly designed blue-and-white hovercraft were an impressive addition to the Spectrum fleet; although their role within the organisation is never made entirely clear.

'Traitor' was also the first episode to incorporate a lengthy flashback scene – in this case, no doubt for the benefit of viewers new to the series, Captain Blue explains how Captain Scarlet became indestructible in the first place.

Teleplay by Tony Barwick
Directed by Alan Perry

As Captain Blue sleeps, Captain Black stealthily prepares his rude awakening.

30 Flight to Atlantica

'We intend to destroy the World Navy complex at Atlantica.'

Assigned to destroy a dangerous drifting wreck, Captains Blue and Ochre succumb to the effects of some Mysteronised champagne and, having had their flight-plan switched by Captain Black, attack the World Navy's Atlantica complex. Incapable of rational thought, the two men are unaware that they are being pursued by Captain Scarlet and Colonel White and plan a repeat attack. But the Spectrum chief determines to stop them, even if it means shooting them out of the sky!

An amusing episode and one which will be of particular interest to *Thunderbirds* fans, as it features an instrumental version of the song 'The Dangerous Game', which was sung by Lady Penelope in the story 'The Cham Cham'.

Teleplay by Tony Barwick
Directed by Leo Eaton

A fleet of flying saucers surrounds Cloudbase. Have the Mysterons finally come to Earth?

Dazed and confused, Captain Blue finds himself in an apparently deserted Cloudbase.

High on Mysteronised champagne, Captains Blue and Ochre prepare to bomb the Atlantica missile complex.

31 Attack on Cloudbase

'We will destroy Cloudbase.'

When Symphony Angel is shot down over the desert, it seems that the Mysterons have finally launched an all-out attack on Spectrum's headquarters. Saucer-like space craft appear out of nowhere and, as Cloudbase is mercilessly blitzed, Captain Scarlet tries to take off in the only surviving Angel aircraft.

A tense and exciting episode which is guaranteed to keep the viewer guessing. As the story draws to a close, it appears that the Mysterons have won the war. The denouement, however, reveals that this is not the case!

Teleplay by Tony Barwick
Directed by Ken Turner

32 The Inquisition

'One of the members of Spectrum will betray you all.'

Having drunk some drugged coffee, Captain Blue awakes in what appears to be a deserted Cloudbase control room. Colonel White is nowhere to be seen and, sitting at his desk, is a man named Colgan, who claims to be from Spectrum Intelligence. Colgan informs Captain Blue that he has been missing for three months and, in order to prove his identity, demands the secret Spectrum cypher codes.

An unusual final episode which relies heavily upon flashbacks to earlier episodes – in particular, an eight-minute long sequence from 'Crater 101'. Rather intriguing, however, is the scene in which, to escape his captors, Blue leaps through a glass portal, and the viewer is afforded a brief glimpse of what must be the back of the control room set.

Teleplay by Tony Barwick
Directed by Ken Turner

'HOLD ON, I CAN SEE SOME WIRES!'

'The Magnacopter's clear, let him have it.'

A sudden burst of machine-gun fire reminded Captain Scarlet that, although Symphony Angel and the conference delegates were now safe, he himself was still within range of Goddard and the armour-piercing shells that had threatened to cut the aircraft to pieces on take-off.

Twisting the directional control of his jet-pack, Scarlet moved forwards at full speed. Behind the machine gun, Goddard spotted him and brought the great weapon to bear. Desperately Scarlet loosed off a couple of shots, but they went wide and he knew that it was hopeless.

The machine gun spat fire in his direction, and he felt the impact and searing pain as a volley of cahelium-tipped bullets tore into his body. Agonised, he released his grip on the jet-pack controls and, like a broken doll, crashed to the floor. The last thing he saw, before unconsciousness claimed him, was the turret of Glengarry Castle erupting like a volcano and hurling shattered blocks of masonry into the sky.

That was how it appeared on November 10th 1967 when the episode 'The Trap' had its TV premiere. But how did 'The Trap' come into being? For the answer, we must journey back to January 1967 when Tony Barwick was assembling the scripts for the series. Barwick, a former computer programmer who had script-edited the last six episodes of *Thunderbirds*, had a small office at the studios of Century 21 and it was here that most of his work was done; meeting and briefing potential writers, editing their finished scripts and writing episodes of his own.

Barwick needed writers who understood the technicalities of writing for puppets, as opposed to flesh and blood actors, and was particularly keen to employ Alan Pattillo, who had acted as script-editor on the first 26 episodes of *Thunderbirds*. Although he was now working on other projects as film-editor, Pattillo was happy to get involved, even though he could only spare enough time to write one script.

With the format of the series already well established, Pattillo was simply given a location and

A jet-propelled Captain Scarlet prepares to shoot it out with Goddard.

asked to write a script around it. The setting for the story, the remote Glengarry Castle, didn't come as a surprise to him because, as he remembers today, 'Gerry always liked to have a Scottish subject in his series!'

Once Pattillo had delivered the finished script, Tony Barwick discussed it with Producer Reg Hill and the various department heads. As Gerry Anderson describes it, 'the whole thing is done with military precision'; therefore, in order to locate and iron out any potential difficulties, each department head looked at the script from their own point of view.

Supervising Art Director Bob Bell defines his job as, 'visualising the backgrounds against which the characters perform. I supervised the working drawings of the interiors which went to the Construction Manager, and then watched the set construction, working with my assistants on the details of the interior design and furnishings.'

Puppet Co-ordinator Mary Turner was responsible for 'casting' the puppets who would

The delegates congregate in the Banquetting Hall of Glengarry Castle. With ten working puppets all in the same shot, this was a time-consuming and difficult scene to film.

play Morton (the caretaker of Glengarry Castle) and the two Mysteron villains: Air Commodore Goddard and his pilot, Holt. For the part of Morton, Mary chose to use a puppet whose face was based on that of Robert Mitchum. As one of the more successful 'guest players', this rugged-faced puppet can be seen, re-costumed, in several episodes, including 'Fire at Rig 15' as the Rig foreman, and 'Spectrum Strikes Back' as Dr Giardelo.

This script provided an additional complication with scenes which called for the ten members of the World Air Conference to be seen in shot at the same time. Since the series was filming two episodes at once on separate stages, duplicate puppets of Captain Scarlet and Captain Blue were kept on both stages, but the supporting players (known as revamps) had to be juggled carefully between both stages. Quite apart from the large number of puppets, these crowd scenes would call for several new military uniforms to be designed, or adapted from others, by Wardrobe Mistress Iris Richens.

At the same time, Production Manager Frank Hollands was checking over the script to see what equipment would be needed for which scenes on which particular stage. Although comparing film production with a factory production line sounds unglamorous, Gerry Anderson points out that 'you could hardly come into a studio of a hundred technicians and say, 'I'm sorry guys but we haven't got the next set ready so can you all go home for a week.'

That weekend, Reg Hill would meet up with the small cast of voice actors at Anvil Films Recording Studio in Denham. Liz Morgan recalls that 'Cy Grant used to pick me up *very* early in the morning, since we both lived in Notting Hill at the time, and we'd drive out to Denham.' With the technical side of the recordings supervised by Anvil's Douglas Hurring, the Century 21 crew would record several episodes in one day.

Because the voices were just one element of what would eventually be a very visual production, this meant that the recording sessions were quite different from an ordinary radio play and the actors needed quite a lot of guidance from Hill or Gerry Anderson. Gerry Anderson explains: 'If you are making a normal feature film or television programme, then the actor knows: "I am running up the stairs, therefore I am out of breath. I am

Captain Scarlet, Goddard and Morton in the Banquetting Hall of Glengarry Castle.

projecting my voice sixty yards across a courtyard. I am falling out of a plane while I am screaming" – he knows the situation. But, of course, when you pre-record the dialogue for a programme, they don't necessarily know how it is going to be filmed. So, for that reason, I always made sure that I was in attendance.'

Actor Ed Bishop, who gave voice to Captain Blue, remembers the sessions well. 'It was very interesting to watch the five or six permanent members of the cast because, after a while, we began to take them very seriously and we'd argue among ourselves and say "Well, my character would never say that!" and often we would have to remind ourselves that we were just recording a children's programme!'

Day one of filming at the Century 21 studio in Slough, and the small army of technicians start work on the 'teaser' – the short scene before the main titles designed to excite the interest of the viewer and make him watch on.

Escorted by Melody Angel, a World Airforce jet flies across a stormy night sky. Lightning illuminates the scene and, as the storm worsens, a fierce bolt of lightning forks from the heavens, striking the aircraft and causing a dramatic explosion. Out of control, the blazing aircraft plummets from the sky, hits the rugged, wooded terrain and explodes. As torrential rain sweeps the smouldering wreckage, the familiar Mysteron circles appear and drift slowly across the bloodied bodies of Goddard and Holt.

Working on a small, dimly-lit set, the equally small 'Flying Unit' take care of the shots of Melody Angel's aircraft and the XQR jet. Attached to thin but strong wires, the two aircraft are suspended in front of a painted backdrop. By rolling the scenery back, the illusion of forward motion is achieved, without having to move either plane so much as an inch. The effect is further enhanced by technicians who stand just out of shot, spraying water and wafting clouds of smoke on to the set from a smoke gun.

Satisfied that the results look convincing, the director moves on to the next shot; that of the lightning strike. Although distant lightning is simulated by the flashing of an arc welder, forked lightning is a different matter altogether. A realistic effect would be impossible to create live in the studio so the lightning will have to be superimposed over the shot by a process known as optical printing.

On the director's cue, a small explosive charge attached to the hidden side of the plane is detonated. Smoke and flames billow from a tube of Jetex fuel pellets fastened to the side of the model. As the smoke is blown backwards by an out of shot fan, the camera is tilted at a steep angle to give the impression that the aircraft is diving towards the ground.

Goddard's jet approaches Cloudbase. An effective shot, achieved by the Flying Unit, unfortunately cut from the finished episode.

Bound and gagged, Captain Scarlet is helpless as the Mysteronized Goddard contacts Cloudbase – using Scarlet's voice!

An unusual publicity shot of Melody Angel, but it does illustrate the unique mechanism which allowed the puppet to be controlled from below.

On the model stage, the sequence is completed by the special effects unit, under the direction of Shaun Whitaker-Cooke. Again trailing fire and smoke, the XQR aircraft slides down a wire towards the rocky mountainside, which is the floor of the set. Although not apparent from the camera's point of view, the foreground is actually separate from the background, leaving a gap between the two just large enough for the plane to fall into. As soon as the plane disappears from sight, carefully positioned petrol gel explosives on the foreground set are ignited. It requires precision timing, but it means that the aircraft can be 'destroyed', whilst, in fact, it remains undamaged. An expensive and highly detailed prop can then be modified and re-used in a later episode.

No sooner has the explosion been captured on film than Whitaker-Cooke shouts 'cut!' and, almost immediately, a couple of technicians rush on to the set with fire extinguishers, to stop the whole thing going up in flames! As the smoke clears, the unit begin to prepare for the next shot – the sequence in which Melody Angel, flying low over the trees, spots the wreckage of the crashed jet. Before any more filming can take place, however, the camera must be carefully dusted down, in order to remove any dust particles thrown up by the explosion, and lubricated, in order to stop the works from seizing up during the high speeds at which it must operate whilst recording special effects shots.

On one of the two puppet stages, a stringless Melody Angel sits in the cockpit of her aircraft, while puppeteer Judith Morgan operates her from below. The unique under-puppet mechanism allows Melody to move convincingly, whilst enclosed within her cockpit. Without this device, such close-up shots as this would have been impossible, as a hole would have to have been made in the roof of the cockpit for the strings to pass through – a hole which would have been difficult to hide from the all-seeing lens of the camera. As director Alan Perry announces a 'wrap', work on the 'teaser' is complete.

Eight thirty the following morning and everyone is preparing for another hard day. On the main puppet stage, a large and well-lit set has been erected – the main control room of Cloudbase. On a raised section of the stage, Colonel White sits behind his circular desk. Below him, sitting before his intricate control console, is Lieutenant Green. The scene being shot requires Green to report to the Colonel whilst moving towards him in his special travelling chair. Hidden from view, just behind Colonel White's desk, a technician slowly pulls the moving walkway to which the Lieutenant's chair is attached. On the overhead bridge, puppet operator Peter Johns matches the Lieutenant's speed, whilst carefully pulling the strings which will give movement to the puppet's arms and head.

An amusing sight, unseen by the programme's viewers, is the caps usually worn by Captains Scarlet and Blue, seeming to hover a couple of feet above their heads. As Puppet Supervisor Christine Glanville explains: 'The caps had to be threaded on to the wires, which were then attached to the puppeteers' hand controls. It would have been a complicated process to have removed the caps completely, when they weren't required, so instead, we simply moved them up out of shot and used insulating tape to hold them in place!'

With the bridge puppeteers positioned eight feet above their respective puppets, the task of making the various characters appear to look at each other during conversation is not an easy one. However, much of the hit-and-miss element of the early shows has been ironed out, thanks to the development of a system known as 'Add-a-Vision'. A very small, closed-circuit view-finder is attached to the camera, allowing everyone on the set, including the bridge puppeteers, to enjoy a 'camera-eye view' of the proceedings.

As the Cloudbase scenes are being shot, the set of the castle interior is being lit on the other puppet stage, under the supervision of Lighting Cameraman Paddy Seal whose job it is to deceive the camera, with careful positioning of lights, to produce a sense of depth and realism. Christine Glanville recalls that 'Gerry always insisted that the eyes of the puppets should be lit to make them look alive. So the lighting cameraman had to position his little key lights in front of them, and of course, if we moved the heads too far to one side, one of the eyes would "go out".'

Several 1000-watt lights hang from the gantry; each one is carefully trained on a different part of the set; this has the effect of producing 'real' shadows, thus exaggerating the natural perspective of the scene. Wall-paintings, suits of armour, the main banqueting table, they all have to be carefully and individually lit – there's even a smaller 120-watt Fresnel behind the window,

The massive and highly detailed model of Cloudbase stands ready for the cameras.

creating the illusion of daylight. The process can take hours; far too long for the puppeteers to hold Captain Scarlet and the others in position, so wooden cut-outs, with the puppet's image painted on, are placed in the relevant positions.

Setting up each shot is a lengthy and meticulous process, as one problem after another arises and has to be solved. Gerry Anderson remembers one problem in particular. 'Imagine a shot with, say, five puppets. You've got everything set up and you're about to go for a take. The puppeteers take up all the slack in the wires and then the camera operator would say, "Hold on, I can see some wires". In would go a guy with a palette of colours and a very fine brush, he would put the brush into shot and the camera operator would literally say "left, left, left – that one there. It's glinting against green." So you'd paint that little bit green, then: "Oh, now the next bit's glinting against black", so you would have to paint the next bit black and this would take forever.'

At last they are ready to go. Surely nothing else can go wrong now. Oh yes it can, as Gerry points out. 'The director would say, "Right, turn over and action", and then an eye-string would break. So, after all that, the whole set-up would have to be canned for twenty minutes to repair the wire. Believe me, it was absolute hell making some of these pictures.'

While all this is happening on the shooting stages, the processed film from previous episodes is being assembled in Century 21's editing suites. Positive black & white 'slash prints' are taken from the negatives and spliced together by the film editor. It is here that the episode really takes shape, as footage from all the different units is cut together to create a smooth-running, 25-minute programme. Once the finished episode has been assembled, the slash print is sent back to the labs where a copy of each selected scene is taken from the original negative.

Once the finished episode has been assembled, the soundtrack has to be added. Together with Music Editor George Randall, Composer Barry Gray views the two separate reels of film which make up the completed episode through a moviola. Using a stopwatch, they decide exactly where each passage of music should begin and end. Working from his home studio in Esher, Surrey, Gray creates the unusual electronic sound effects and music using such instruments as the Baldwin electronic harpsichord and the Ondes Martenot (an electronic device which produces high-pitched wails similar to that on The Beach Boys' hit 'Good Vibrations'). Together with tape recorders, which can slow down or reverse these noises, Barry is able to create the bizarre oscillating sounds associated with the Mysterons. Having already recorded the theme music at two earlier sessions, Barry will then travel to Anvil Studios in Denham where, with a small orchestra, he will record much of the incidental music for the episode. Recorded on to ¼-inch tape, the music and sound effects are taken back to Anvil Studios and, under the careful control of Anvil's Ken Scrivener, mixed with the dialogue track and transferred to the finished film.

The final day's shooting and all that remains is the episode's climax, a dramatic scene in which Captain Scarlet confronts Goddard amid the battlements of Glengarry Castle. A highly

Close-ups of real hands were inserted at key points in the programme for added realism. Here, stand-ins act out the scene in which Captain Scarlet is surprised by Goddard.

High on the battlements, Goddard has the Magnacopter pinned down. Can Captain Scarlet distract his attention for long enough to allow the delegates to escape?

detailed set has been built, which incorporates a battlement wall, a rough, earth-strewn floor and a curved and windowed turret. Positioned at one end of the set is the Mysteronised Goddard, his face set, gripping the handles of a powerful, heavy-duty machine gun. At the other end of the set, strapped into his jet-pack, is Captain Scarlet.

As well as his supporting wires, Captain Scarlet has now been fitted with an additional wire and thin rubber pipe which will allow his hand-held gun to fire. The carefully concealed rubber pipe carries a supply of gas to the nozzle of the gun. An electric impulse is generated and travels down the wire, igniting the gas and making the gun appear to fire. The machine gun works on a similar principle, although obviously uses a much larger gas jet.

With Special Effects Director Derek Meddings busy on the model stage, Special Effects Assistant Ian Wingrove attaches a strip of Cortex explosive to the mock granite wall, behind which Captain Scarlet is seen to hide. As Director Alan Perry shouts 'Action!', Goddard opens fire and, as Scarlet is pulled back by his operator, the strip of Cortex is ignited, giving the impression of a line of bullet holes suddenly appearing in the wall. Moving back into the open and returning fire, Scarlet orders Captain Blue to open up with the

SPV rocket. It is then that his luck seems to run out. Hovering a few feet off the ground, Scarlet is without cover and, as Goddard opens fire, the Spectrum agent is caught in a stream of bullets. Now wearing the 'grimacing head' first seen in 'The Mysterons', Scarlet is seen to clutch his bleeding stomach, before crashing to the floor. To achieve the effect, Floor Puppeteer Rowena White takes hold of Scarlet, his strings now slack, and, upon the director's command, throws him to the floor. The puppet is sturdy enough to withstand the fall without any damage and Alan Perry is satisfied that he has got the result he wants.

On the model stage, meanwhile, Derek Meddings and his assistant Ian Wingrove are wiring up the scale-model of Glengarry Castle for what will be a truly explosive climax! Having packed the tower with petrol gel, Meddings and his assistant don protective helmets and retreat to a safe distance. Then the high-speed camera rolls and the firing button is depressed. All at once the tower of Glengarry Castle explodes brilliantly, balsa wood and chunks of polystyrene masonry being thrown in all directions. It takes only a couple of seconds and in the studio it looks spectacular enough but when slowed down and combined with the appropriate sound effects, it will look just like the real thing!

'THIS INDESTRUCTIBLE MAN

WILL SHOW WHAT HE'S WORTH.'

Captain Scarlet premiered in the days before home video recorders. Fans had just half an hour to see the show before it was over for the rest of the week. There was only one way in which a truly dedicated fan could fill the hours until the following week's thrilling episode, and that was to collect the merchandise. Captain Scarlet was created with merchandising potential very much in mind. 'Make it a Captain Scarlet Christmas' was Century 21's slogan and the British toy industry responded with enthusiasm.

Lines Brothers, the massive combine responsible for a third of British toys, led the stampede with their Dinky subsidiary. One of the best-selling Dinkys of all time was their metallic blue SPV. Boasting an intricate door mechanism which opened sideways to lower Captain Scarlet to the ground, the 16-cm-long model was almost completely faithful to the TV original. Despite its many working parts (such as a missile-launcher) the SPV was robust enough to survive the toughest playtime crash. Dinky had enough pride in the SPV to put it on the cover of their 1968 catalogue – itself a collector's item today.

Dinky's 14-cm MSV was an attractive as the SPV but offered less in the way of entertainment. Once the owner had flipped up the cream 'gull-wing' doors and pulled down the red plastic ramps, there was little to do except ponder over the plastic crate of 'radioactive isotopes' which came with the MSV. Dinky's metallic red Spectrum Patrol Car (Spectrum Saloon in the series) offered only an 'engine-noise mechanism' as a special feature. Nevertheless, both the SPC and

the MSV are today almost as collectable as the SPV. In pristine condition, with the original boxes, the set would cost nearly three hundred pounds.

Pedigree Dolls was another Lines Brothers subsidiary which produced three figures based on the series. The 12-inch Captain Scarlet doll was made in the style of Pedigree's 'Tommy Gunn'

Just some of the many and varied items of merchandise.

soldier doll with a fabric costume and articulated limbs. The concept of the doll for boys was still very fresh in 1967, but the Captain Scarlet doll was doomed from the start. Unlike the original GI Joe and Action Man, the doll had no additional costumes or equipment; not even a jet pack to fly around with. The only enemy he could fight would be a Mysteronised Tommy Gunn.

Pedigree also issued two smaller dolls, roughly the same size as today's GI Joe toys. Captain Scarlet and Destiny Angel were moulded from soft rubber with a wire skeleton. Their costumes were very detailed; Scarlet's cap included a perspex visor and pull-down microphone, and at his waist was a gunbelt and tiny pistol. Destiny Angel had a removable plastic helmet and removable artificial hair. Sadly, these very details meant that the dolls were quite fragile. Their arms and legs had a spindly appearance and were correspondingly delicate.

The third 'big-name' from Lines Brothers was Tri-Ang which issued a 'Captain Scarlet' set to add to its 'Minic' electric car-racing game (very similar to Scalextric). The rival firm of Rovex

Large plastic replicas from *Century 21.*

Industries also produced a similar 'Captain Scarlet Escape and Capture' set, which came with four pieces of track, an electric SPC and a Mysteronised sports car. Unlike the dolls, these car games were deliberately intended to be added on to an existing game.

In much the same spirit, Timpo Toys, who sold a fantastic range of plastic cowboys and soldiers at pocket-money prices, produced three Spectrum figures. Basically, the same detailed, 2-inch body with uniforms moulded in scarlet, white and green, the toys lent themselves to any number of battles with Mysteronised cowboys. Their other selling point was that they were almost in scale with the plastic Spectrum vehicles made by Century 21 Toys. At almost a foot in length, the Century 21 vehicles were much more delicate than their Dinky counterparts but featured additional gimmicks. The SPV incorporated roof-hatch ejector seats for Captain Scarlet and Captain Blue, while the wing mirrors of the SPC triggered missile launchers in the headlights of the car. Dwarfing both these toys was the Angel interceptor, which came with its own 'slot-in' friction motor. Definitely in the 'broken by Boxing Day' category, they were made from a much more fragile polystyrene than that used for present-day toy production. As a collector's item an Angel Interceptor in warehouse condition can sell for as much as two hundred pounds.

For those fans who actually wanted to 'be' Captain Scarlet, Century 21 Toys produced a polythene playsuit and a range of futuristic water pistols. For the girls, they commissioned Angels' Beauty and Jewellery sets as well as a transparent pendant which carried photos of the Spectrum Captains. Airfix also licensed a plastic construction kit of the Angel interceptor, made with the attention to detail for which Airfix was renowned. In fact, the Angel interceptor was probably the most enduring piece of Captain Scarlet merchandising, still on sale in chain stores until the early 1980s.

Quite apart from toys, Washington Potteries issued attractive cups decorated with transfers of Spectrum agents and vehicles, while Lone Star turned out a line of gaudy metal badges. Wonderama concocted a 6-foot wall frieze illustrated with scenes from such episodes as 'Spectrum Strikes Back', and Crown produced full-scale Captain Scarlet wallpaper.

John Waddingtons got in on the act with four 250-piece jigsaws based on colour stills from the series, but ironically, Captain Scarlet only appears on one of the jigsaws. Waddingtons also invented an elaborate Captain Scarlet board game. Played against the map of Europe, it involved four plastic SPCs transporting VIPs to the Spectrum Conference Centre in Yugoslavia. Moves were determined by a roll of the dice and

'Mysteron Cards' which required agents to miss a turn or return to base. The box artwork carries pictures of both Captain Scarlet and Destiny Angel. In fact, Destiny Angel, who was based on actress Ursula Andress, features in much of the merchandising, even though she did not have a particularly prominent role in the TV show.

Fans with a sweet tooth could buy Captain Scarlet biscuits with photographs of the Spectrum agents printed on the foil wrappers. Anglo bubble-gum also issued a set of sixty-six collector's cards – the front of each card showed either a photograph or drawing based on the series while the reverse made up a giant jigsaw painting by Ron Embleton, who had also painted the end-title sequence for the TV show. Barratt's Sweet Cigarettes (known to today's more healthy generation as Candy Sticks) issued a set of fifty smaller cards and also sponsored a special 24-page Spectrum Handbook, produced by Century 21 Publications and only available by mail order.

With his ice-cool nerve, it was inevitable that Captain Scarlet would promote Lyons-Maid's new Orbit ice lolly. J. Walter Thompson commissioned Century 21 to make a special TV advert for Orbit in which Captain Scarlet defended the newly completed Post Office Tower from Mysterons by turning the ice-lolly into a Mysteron-seeking missile.

Captain Scarlet was a natural successor to Virgil Tracy on the Kellogg's Sugar Smacks packet, and the loyalty of young consumers was assured by the free gifts. In-pack premiums included a set of small metal badges illustrated with the faces of Spectrum agents and snap-together plastic models (about an inch long) of the ever-popular Spectrum vehicles.

When it came to kits, nobody did it more comprehensively than the Japanese. Imai of Japan initiated a massive range of kits which were later repackaged in Canada and the United States. The Spectrum helicopter, Cloudbase and the Swift Removals SPV Transporter were just three of the items which Imai added to the usual range of character and vehicle merchandising.

Back in Britain, pyjamas, slacks, balloons, kites, slippers and a sketch pad were added to the merchandising list. The House of Romney's

A selection of the many books which were produced to tie in with the series.

'Captain Scarlet Asteroid Talc' is probably the most obscure item of merchandising while the award for the most ephemeral goes to the water transfers produced by Tower Press of London. Water transfers were generally sold in sweet shops during school lunch hours and as with stamps were torn off a larger folio. The individual pictures were based on paintings by Jim Watson and Malcolm Stokes and could be applied to the skin by wetting the back of the transfer under a tap. The transfers were produced in such large quantities that it is still relatively easy to buy a sheet from dealers today.

Slightly less common is the original *Captain Scarlet* annual, published in 1967 to coincide with the TV premiere. For many years, this annual was the *Scarlet* fan's bible, containing articles on Spectrum, its personnel, vehicles and enemies. Devised by Todd Sullivan and Angus Allan of Century 21 Publications the book is very much a snapshot of the original Captain Scarlet concept. In every comic strip, for instance, Captain Scarlet's 'sixth sense' causes him to 'sweat and sway whenever he comes near a Mysteron'. The TV shows quickly abandoned the 'sixth sense' concept because it gave the scriptwriters too many problems and yet the comic strips, with colour artwork by Jim Watson, Keith Watson (of *Dan Dare* fame) and Ron Turner (of *The Daleks*) demonstrate just how imaginatively the gimmick can be used. The strips also show the SPV power pack being adapted for use as a high-powered drill and one-man helicopter; ideas which are discussed in the pilot script but never actually used in the TV show. For these reasons, and Roger Perry's excellent design work, the annual is well worth hunting down.

Century 21 Publications also released 20 large-format booklets which included painting, sticker-fun, dot-to-dot and puzzle books for both *Scarlet* and *The Angels*. Two other books in the *Scarlet* range gave buyers a chance to build cardboard cut-out models of Cloudbase and the Spectrum vehicles, while *The Angels* range featured cut-out clothes dolls based on Destiny, Harmony, and Rhapsody. Last but not least, both *Scarlet* and *The Angels* had their own hardback storybooks illustrated in colour by Jim Watson.

In addition to their own-label books, Century 21 also packaged three novels for Armada books.

Written under Century 21's house pseudonym of John Theydon, the first book, 'Captain Scarlet and the Mysterons', is a fast-moving epic in which the Mysterons use a weather control machine to hammer the World Government into submission. This allows the author to tackle scenes which are beyond the budget of the TV show, such as a tropical rainstorm engulfing the crowds in a futuristic Trafalgar Square. As in the annual, the problem of Captain Scarlet's 'sixth sense' is tackled head on. Captain Black warns a Mysteronised World Space Patrol engineer that Scarlet can

Captain Scarlet was regularly featured on the cover of *TV 21*.

detect their unique radiation so the engineer fools Scarlet by donning his radiation-proof spacesuit.

Less satisfying is Spectrum File No.2, 'Captain Scarlet and the Silent Saboteur', a fairly uneventful tale concerning the disappearance of the highly advanced *Oceanus X* submarine and a plot by the Mysterons to destroy the world's circle of energy-producing Thermic Power Stations.

Apart from issuing *Captain Scarlet* material, Century 21 Publications had the weekly comics to create. Ron Embleton's *Captain Scarlet* comic strip continued in the centrespread of *TV21* with Spectrum battling Mysteronised WASP (from *Stingray*) and WSP (from *Fireball XL5*) agents. The Spectrum symbol was incorporated into the *TV21* masthead, and in the letters page readers were encouraged to mail in reports of local Mysteron activity. *TV21* even offered readers the chance to join Spectrum's junior division – the Shades. This ambitious operation began by dividing the map of Britain into 12 colour-coded areas. Each area was commanded by a Spectrum Captain to whom readers could report (additional characters such as Captain Cream and Lt Sepia being created for both the Shades and the comic). Readers could get their first Shade membership card, free of charge, just by writing to *TV21*. Shades then had the chance to trade in that card for one of a higher rank (a different colour naturally) if they passed an examination printed in the comic. It was a great idea; they had the cards printed up in all the colours of the rainbow, and the exam entries began flooding in. Only then did the *TV21* staff realise that they didn't have time to check the exam forms. In previous years, competition entries had been processed by a separate department and even that had been a much simpler task then checking 20 questions on each form.

Although they made sure that every correct entrant eventually received his or her new card, the *TV21* staff decided to drastically revise the promotion structure of the Shades organisation. Readers were distracted by a devastating storyline in the *Captain Scarlet* strip. Chris Spencer, who was editing *TV21* at the time, had noticed that most of the readers' letters seemed to come from 'Area Purple'; what is now the Yorkshire Television region. Since toy manufacturers also reported high sales in this area the explanation

seems to have been that there were more children in Area Purple than in any of the other regions. Whatever the cause, *TV21* swung into action with a story in which Captain Purple was promoted from answering Shades letters just long enough to die saving an underwater city.

Meanwhile, *Captain Scarlet* had changed the face of *TV 21* forever. The newspaper front page, which had made the comic so unique, was replaced by the opening panels of the *Captain Scarlet* comic strip. Boosted to four pages a week (two of them in black and white) the feature was now too much work for one artist alone. Ron Embleton was joined on the strip by several artists, each one tackling a different three-part story. Mike Noble, from the *Zero X* strip, contributed several 'Bond-style' adventures, featuring massive gunbattles and cross-continuity with the other *TV21*

'Hold it right there!' Stuart Evans' beautifully detailed Captain Scarlet sets his sights on Captain Black.

strips. Former *Dan Dare* artist Keith Watson contributed elegant views of 21st century London in a nightmare storyline about one of Scarlet's closest relatives being Mysteronised. Another *Dan Dare* graduate, Don Harley, drew the Captain Purple storyline. Even Frank Bellamy found a big enough hole in his *Thunderbirds* schedule to draw a *Captain Scarlet* cover (leaving Jim Watson to draw the interior pages). Working from scripts by Angus Allan and Scott Goodall, the artists produced an athletic version of Captain Scarlet that is today as fondly remembered as the series itself.

Now that they were TV stars in their own right, the Angels were used to promote the *Lady Penelope* comic in the TV adverts, and editor Gillian Allan boosted their comic strip to a two page length with guest appearances by Captain Blue and Captain Black. The comic also featured *The Spectrum*, a one-page strip by Tom Kerr, about the 'real-life' adventures of the group who sang the *Captain Scarlet* theme song. City Magazines, which distributed and co-published *TV21*, also published a comic called *TV Tornado*, which featured reprints of American comic strips and text features by *Marvelman* creator Mick Anglo. When *Solo* was cancelled, it was 'absorbed' by *TV Tornado* and Century 21 supplied the merged comic with a strip based on 'The Mysterons'. In fact, it was virtually a retread of *The Daleks* strip which had appeared on the back of *TV21* for its first two years. Each week, the 'giant computer' which ruled the Mysteron complex would blow up one of the Martian buildings and recreate it as a flying saucer. The Mysteron craft would then fly to another planet, where the atmosphere would cause the formless beings to 'take on their ancient Mysteron shape'. In the form of giant crystals, with a 'death ray' eye slit, the Mysterons would commence exterminating the alien races. Apart from the use of the Zero-X craft and the Martian City of Kahra, the strip had very little to do with either the Anderson universe or the TV series.

In the days before home video, the final piece of merchandising was perhaps the most satisfying. Century 21 released several 7-inch Extended Play records through ATV's Pye Records. Recorded at the same time as the actual film soundtracks, the first two 'mini-albums' were simply re-edited versions of TV episodes. The next four records

The personnel and vehicles illustrated on this specification sheet, are featured in 'Captain Scarlet and the Mysterons', the T.V. series by Gerry and Sylvia Anderson.

were original scripts, produced in the style of radio plays by Dennis Skelton, and featuring most of the original cast members. 'Captain Scarlet and the Mysterons', by Angus Allan, gives Scarlet the task of parachuting aboard a Mysteronised jet, while 'Captain Scarlet Versus Captain Black' by *TV21* script editor Richard O'Neill features Captain Black's attempt to lure Scarlet into a duel with electrode guns.

A rare specifications sheet issued to toymakers before the series was broadcast.

Century 21 sales reps meeting, August 1967: 'Okay Boys. Let's make this a *Captain Scarlet* Christmas!'

THE FINAL BATTLE AND BEYOND . . .

As if to underline the merchandising slogan about making it a 'Captain Scarlet Christmas', the Christmas Day 1967 edition of ATV's game show *The Golden Shot* had a Captain Scarlet theme. A forerunner of Central TV's *Bullseye*, using crossbows instead of darts, the show was hosted by Bob Monkhouse, who had played the voice of Zero X navigator Brad Newman in the film *Thunderbirds Are Go!* The two hostesses, Carol Dilworth and Anne Aston, were outfitted in Angel uniforms, and the Spectrum pop group made one of their few live appearances in the musical break. The celebrity contestant, firing a crossbow on behalf of a disabled viewer, was none other than Captain Scarlet, relaying instructions by satellite from Cloudbase. To ensure that Captain Scarlet could exchange seasonal banter with Bob Monkhouse, the dialogue for the puppet was spoken 'live'. Francis Matthews recalls that 'I supplied my voice, as the show was being done, from the safe confines of a recording booth, well away from Bob!'

ATV Midlands broadcast the last episode of *Captain Scarlet and the Mysterons* on Tuesday May 14th, 1968, and by now, Century 21 Publications were already concentrating on their next production, *Joe 90*. As Gerry himself says, 'After the shock with *Thunderbirds* being cancelled, I'd just assumed that Scarlet would be cancelled after one series.'

TV21 continued to run the Captain Scarlet strips on the cover and inside pages, and in the October 19th edition it appeared that the Mysterons had actually conceded defeat. As the Mysterons complex shut down, Captain Black regained his old personality and President Younger disbanded Spectrum. The Angels and SPVs were turned over to the WAAF, Captains Blue and Scarlet transferred to the WSP as pilots of XL19, and Captain Black retired to a country cottage. Of course, there was only one way (apart from a dream) that the story could be concluded. It was all a cunning ruse! The Mysterons returned and Spectrum was hastily reconvened, with the help of Steve Zodiac, flying a new space-time machine.

In Autumn 1968, Captain Scarlet starred in the *TV21* annual and his second and last ninety-six-page annual. *TV2000*, a Dutch comic which reprinted the Century 21 strips had faithfully reproduced the Five Julias (Angels) and Voorpagina (front page) strips that introduced Spectrum.

Cloudbase goes down. Is this the end of Spectrum's floating HQ?

'Have I ever told you about the time I saved Colonel White's life?' Symphony and Melody exchange a knowing glance – they've heard it all before!

89

Unfortunately, the Dutch TV service only screened six episodes of Captain Scarlet, so the translated version of the comic strip was the greatest exposure most Netherlanders got to Captain Scarlet.

Meanwhile, in Britain the expense of equipping new colour studios was compounded by a Government tax on advertising revenue, and forced ATV to cut costs. Century 21 merchandising was streamlined; the toy company was closed down, and the publishing company was sold. Since City Magazines was still in operation at that time, *TV21* continued to appear, although the Century 21 content was gradually phased out. On July 12th the Mysterons were driven away after a scientist discovered a method of beaming cosmic rays down at their Martian settlement. Although they vowed revenge, they left Captain Black behind – a lifeless corpse. For the last few weeks Captain Scarlet continued as a kind of indestruc-

Destiny and Symphony prepare to leave Cloudbase in their rather attractive demob suits.

tible cop fighting Arcturan criminals. On September 6th 1969 *TV21* was closed down. Ironically, *Captain Scarlet* was already being repeated by some ITV companies, and his fight with the Mysterons would continue to be broadcast throughout 1970.

Although *TV21* had been cancelled, the liquidation of Century 21 publications had come too late to prevent the preparation of a combined *Thunderbirds* and *Captain Scarlet* annual. In the same format as previous annuals, it featured comic strips, cutaways of the Cloudbase computer and sick bay, plus a map of Mars which attempted to tie together continuity of *Thunderbirds are Go!* and *Captain Scarlet*. Century 21 had also packaged a 21st Century diary for Letts, which revealed that Captain Black and the Mysterons negotiated a peace treaty with the World President some years after the series ended.

In late 1970, Arthur Thorne, the head of Polystyle Publications, decided that the Anderson characters were too good to waste and he asked Dennis Hooper, the former art director of *TV21* to edit a new comic called *Countdown*. The first issue of *Countdown* came out in February 1971. Although Gerry Anderson's *UFO* and *Doctor Who* (with Jon Pertwee) were the main features, Captain Scarlet starred in a one-page strip drawn by John Cooper, the artist who had illustrated the final *TV21* episodes. The strip was very faithful to the TV concept with the Mysterons and Captain Black at full strength. After the first serial ended, Captain Scarlet became an irregular feature, illustrated by Malcolm Stokes and Brian Lewis.

Captain Scarlet also featured in the 1971 *Thunderbirds* annual (actually made up from the unpublished pages of the last *TV21* annual). In April 1972, *Countdown* became *TV Action*, with much of the science-fiction content being replaced by the likes of *Hawaii Five-O* and *The Protectors*. *Captain Scarlet* continued to appear, however, by way of reprints from *TV21*.

Although Granada, HTV and Tyne Tees continued to broadcast *Scarlet* well into 1972, this would be the last time that the show would be repeated for many years. The fact that *Thunderbirds* was re-screened as early as 1976 led to a rumour that Captain Scarlet had been banned by the ITV companies for its violence. This rumour was lent credence when special interest groups in

Spectrum's gang of four in civvy gear prepare to address the crowd at an early Fanderson convention.

America forced local TV stations to ban such 'violent' cartoons as *Batman* and *Superman*. Yet although British pressure groups have criticised everything from *Grange Hill* to *Doctor Who*, a lengthy search has uncovered no recorded criticism of *Captain Scarlet*.

This does not surprise psychologist Dr George Sik who says, 'kids are actually very sophisticated viewers, far more mature than adults tend to think. The idea of an indestructible hero will be interpreted in the context of the kind of programme *Captain Scarlet* is. Myths abound of children jumping out of windows and locking themselves in fridges, imitating the adventures of indestructible heroes but such instances are extremely rare.'

Stingray comic artist Lynn Simpson recalls, 'It never really occurred to me to ask how the Mysterons' powers worked or why Captain Scarlet was indestructible. All I wanted to know was if Captain Scarlet would get killed and if he'd come back to life at the end of the episode.'

In the early 1980s, the new market of local cable stations in America inspired Robert Mandell of ITC's New York office to repackage several Anderson productions as TV movies under the general title of Super Space Theater. *Captain Scarlet vs The Mysterons* (somewhat perplexingly issued as the second commercial video in Britain) cuts together 'The Mysterons', 'Winged Assassin', 'Seek and Destroy' and 'Attack on Cloudbase'. Britain's 'volume one' was *Revenge of the Mysterons From Mars*, which combines 'Shadow of Fear' with the Lunarville trilogy. A new prologue is delivered by an American Mysteron voice, reporting to the Mysteron High Council in deep space. Apart from that, the story is largely unaltered with the exception of some video laser effects superimposed over the original rocket battles. In Britain, the Super Space Theater productions were never aired on TV, instead being released direct to the fledgling video hire shops (at the time, commercial videotapes were still far too expensive to sell over the counter).

As interest in Gerry's series increased, a group of dedicated fans, led by Pamela Barnes, organised the first UK Gerry Anderson convention.

Held at the Dragonara Hotel in Leeds, 'Fanderson '81' was a three-day event, comprising screenings of selected episodes, a display of original models and personal appearances by Gerry Anderson and the voice of Captain Blue, Ed Bishop. Such was the popularity of the event that the organising committee approached ITC with a view to setting up an authorised fan-club and, a year after the first groundbreaking event, Fanderson – the Official Gerry Anderson Appreciation Society – was born. Eleven years later, under Chris Bentley's leadership, Fanderson has 1,600 members from as far afield as Iceland and Japan.

In 1988, the club issued an Extended Play 7-inch record as part of their yearly membership package. Designed to look like a Century 21 mini-album, the record featured original compositions by Barry Gray, many of which had not been available on record before. Alongside such favourites as the themes from *UFO* and *Thunderbirds*, compilers Ralph Titterton and Steve Kyte had included the Spectrum's 'Captain Scarlet' and 'White as Snow', a light, catchy jazz tune which turned up in the episode of the same name. More recently the second issue of Fanderson's *21st*

David Nightingale's *Century 21* – the indispensible magazine for Gerry Anderson fans of all ages.

It's all over: Captains Scarlet and Blue put their feet up and plan their holiday.

Century Fiction magazine celebrated the 25th anniversary of *Captain Scarlet* with a full-length novella 'Crisis' by Colleen Taylor.

Prior to the formation of Fanderson, Blackpool-based David Nightingale was authorised by ITC to create the first magazine devoted entirely to the world of Century 21. Dave's connection with Gerry Anderson goes back to 1979 when his exhibition in Blackpool needed relocating from the Golden Mile to the Pleasure Beach. 'The only economic way of doing it was to enlist the help of locally based enthusiasts. I was responsible for coordinating the move of the exhibition displays and the construction of the new venue. Philip Rae was responsible for renovating the models and designing the exhibition itself.' Through this Dave became firm friends with Gerry and, in April 1981, the first issue of *SIG* became available. That Spectrum's call-sign should be chosen as the magazine's title is indicative of just how familiar it had become; although as far as Dave's publication was concerned, it stood for 'Supermarionation is Go!'

Out of work and out of luck, Paul Metcalfe drowns his sorrows and hopes for a phone call from Gerry Anderson.

As the publishing concern grew, evolving, ultimately, into today's 'Engale Marketing', so the range of merchandise produced was increased. Calendars and postcards, all featuring Captain Scarlet, have proved to be extremely popular and, between 1988 and 1989, many of the original *TV21* Scarlet strips were re-printed in the glossy *Action 21*. Today, Dave's company publishes *Century 21*, a quarterly successor to *SIG*, edited by Mike Reccia and produced to an impressive professional standard. Dave ensures that regular coverage is given to Captain Scarlet and the Mysterions, which he describes as 'visually stunning and technically practically flawless.'

In 1985, the ITV companies began screening Captain Scarlet on Saturday mornings, and if nothing else, illustrated ITV's contempt for their audience, with episodes being screened out of sequence or slipped, without notice, into schedules when rain interrupted cricket matches. By now, however, Gerry Anderson had begun to receive the recognition denied him in the 1970s. Such varied venues as the Battersea Puppet Centre and the University of Belfast began screening selected episodes of the puppet shows, while the Institute of Contemporary Arts in London mounted a retrospective of Anderson's career including 'The Mysterons'.

By 1987, some of the original viewers of *Captain Scarlet* were old enough to be working in television on Granada's late lamented 'Night Network'. Scheduled for a late-night viewing audience, the series sandwiched five-minute segments of shows like *Batman*, *The Monkees* and *Captain Scarlet* between pop videos and celebrity interviews, while Polygram were now marketing the complete series of *Captain Scarlet* on commercial videotapes. Of course, all episodes of *Captain Scarlet* are going to be reshown on BBC2 during 1993. Following the successes of *Thunderbirds* and *Stingray*, *Captain Scarlet* is bound to be a hit with a whole new generation.

In the quarter of a century since his first appearance, Captain Scarlet has experienced the changing fortunes of all celebrities. A veteran of many battles, this remarkable character has beaten the odds time and time again; has triumphed over an apparently invincible enemy and risen phoenix-like from a graveyard full of forgotten heroes. As the 21st century draws near, Captain Scarlet seems certain to survive. Neither time nor the Mysterons have succeeded in defeating him and it is safe to assume that he will be fighting them both long after his mortal rivals have been laid to rest. Captain Scarlet is, after all, indestructible.

When will I see you again?
The cast enjoy an end-of-
shoot party, oblivious to
Harmony Angel's hovering
helmet!

INDEX